P9-DFK-278

"Don't break any rules on my account."

"Not to worry. But there is something I plan to do on your account."

"Don't do me any favors."

"Actually it's myself I'm concerned about." He picked up his ice cream again and started eating. "It seems the people here in town are all very protective of you. To win their hearts and minds I need to prove myself to you, earn your friendship. And that's exactly what I intend to do."

"Good luck with that." She struggled for a flip attitude, but was pretty sure it didn't work, what with her heart pounding so hard. "I've built up an immunity to nice, charming men."

"Then it's a good thing I'm not nice or charming."

Dear Reader,

How often have you heard the expression "Family—can't live with 'em, can't live without 'em." It's certainly something I've experienced. Although I wouldn't trade my loved ones for anything, that doesn't mean you shouldn't have space.

Dr. Adam Stone understands the saying well, what with his overachieving parents and siblings. He's determined to choose his own path, and that takes him to Blackwater Lake, Montana. He wants small-town life, a place where he can be part of the community. What he doesn't expect is the community to give him the cold shoulder because of another good-looking doctor who "done wrong" Jill Beck, one of their own.

Jill is the town sweetheart and all her friends circle the wagons to protect her from the new doctor. But she has a child to raise and bills to pay. She needs to rent her upstairs apartment, no matter how much she hates the idea of Adam Stone so close. It's not just her heart at risk. Her six-year-old son desperately wants a father, but she's determined to protect them both from a man she believes won't stay.

I had so much fun creating these characters and hope their story will warm your heart as much as it did mine.

Enjoy!

Teresa Southwick

THE DOCTOR AND THE SINGLE MOM

TERESA SOUTHWICK

HARLEQUIN®
entertain, enrich, inspire™

If you purchased this book without a cover you should be aware
that this book is stolen property. It was reported as "unsold and
destroyed" to the publisher, and neither the author nor the
publisher has received any payment for this "stripped book."

Recycling programs
for this product may
not exist in your area.

ISBN-13: 978-0-373-65686-8

THE DOCTOR AND THE SINGLE MOM

Copyright © 2012 by Teresa Southwick

All rights reserved. Except for use in any review, the reproduction
or utilization of this work in whole or in part in any form by any
electronic, mechanical or other means, now known or hereafter
invented, including xerography, photocopying and recording, or in
any information storage or retrieval system, is forbidden without
the written permission of the publisher, Harlequin Enterprises Limited,
225 Duncan Mill Road, Don Mills, Ontario M3B 3K9, Canada.

This is a work of fiction. Names, characters, places and incidents are
either the product of the author's imagination or are used fictitiously, and
any resemblance to actual persons, living or dead, business establishments,
events or locales is entirely coincidental.

This edition published by arrangement with Harlequin Books S.A.

For questions and comments about the quality of this book please contact us
at Customer_eCare@Harlequin.ca.

® and TM are trademarks of Harlequin Enterprises Limited or its corporate
affiliates. Trademarks indicated with ® are registered in the United States Patent
and Trademark Office, the Canadian Trade Marks Office and in other countries.

www.Harlequin.com

Printed in U.S.A.

Books by Teresa Southwick

TERESA SOUTHWICK

lives with her husband in Las Vegas, the city that reinvents itself every day. An avid fan of romance novels, she is delighted to be living out her dream of writing for Harlequin.

To my husband, Tom. I love you—first, last, always.

Chapter One

"I really like what I see."

Adam Stone wasn't just talking about the apartment for rent. The same applied to the pretty lady renting it. Jill Beck was hot, and not just because of all that curly red hair. The thought of asking her out crossed his mind, but that wasn't why he was here. A truck with his stuff was on the way from Dallas to Montana and he needed to find a place to live here in Blackwater Lake before it arrived.

"Isn't this a little too small for you, Dr. Stone?" When Jill settled her brown-eyed gaze on him, he momentarily lost the power of speech.

The two of them were standing in a spacious living room. One window looked out at a dense forest of evergreen trees, and the other had a view of the wide expanse of sparkling blue water known as Blackwater Lake. Only the woman in front of him was a better view than either.

"Call me Adam."

He glanced at the body of water that gave the town one hundred miles north of Billings, Montana, its name. Then he looked around the apartment again. It seemed like just what the doctor ordered. The unit had an eat-in kitchen plus two bedrooms and baths. The walls were painted a light olive-green and trimmed with wide white baseboards that butted up against the pinewood floor. Crown molding highlighted the nine-foot ceilings.

The stairs up to this apartment were located to the side of her front door. He'd seen her place and it was identical to this one, although her walls were painted a particularly sunny shade of yellow that was appealing. He'd thought it suited her, until he turned serious about becoming her tenant. Wariness now replaced her cheery expression.

He folded his arms over his chest and looked down at her. "I'm a single guy. How much room do you think I need?"

"I have a feeling it's more than you can find in my upstairs." The clouds swirling in her beautiful eyes definitely wouldn't drop precipitation in the light-to-moderate range.

Adam could tell he was in for a hard time. A family practice doctor learned to listen, note verbal cues and read between the lines. He was a really good family practice doctor and knew her jeans were in a knot about something. Maybe when they'd climbed the stairs she'd caught him checking out her butt.

It was in his top five, hovering around one or two in the shapeliest category. He was a guy and guys were hardwired to notice girls, especially pretty ones. As far as looks, Jill Beck wasn't in the top ten, but there was something about her. And not just her chest. Yeah, he'd noticed that, too, but had been very careful to look at her face during this conversation.

The positive part of that was appreciating the cute splash of freckles on her upturned nose. But admiring her butt and the freckles on her face wasn't a hanging offense, so he was at a loss about what was bugging her.

Talking was the best way for him to find out. "If I was a family man instead of a family practice doctor, your upstairs would present some space challenges. But that's not the case. I was told it's the best place to rent and I can see why."

"Someone at Mercy Medical Clinic told you about me?"

"Yes." The retiring doctor he was replacing had given him the scoop. Along with two thumbs-up from the receptionist and the nurse.

"Have you looked anywhere else?" she asked.

"I have," he admitted. "But there's not a lot available."

"There are a couple of houses," she said helpfully. "And the Blackwater Lake Lodge probably has a room until you find just what you're looking for."

"Yeah. But the houses aren't as convenient to town and the clinic. The lodge—" He shrugged. "I want to settle somewhere. By process of elimination, that puts this property in the lead."

"Lucky me." Her tone struggled for upbeat but fell way short.

Adam could feel his stubbornness kicking in, and that wasn't necessarily a good thing. "I'd like to rent your apartment, Miss Beck."

If she noticed he didn't call her Jill, she didn't say anything. She shrugged. "The lease is on my desk. I suggest you read it before making a final decision."

There was a warning in the words, but he followed her downstairs to the computer desk tucked into a corner of her living room. This furnished twin of the upstairs apartment gave him an idea how homey it could be.

A chocolate-brown sofa sat in front of the fireplace with a flat-screen TV on the wall over it. The couch partitioned the room into work and relaxation spaces and with warm touches in both. Brass lamps with scalloped shades on tables. In framed pictures covering the walls he recognized the lake outside and the surrounding mountains. Photographs were everywhere. On the desk beside the computer was one of Jill with a little boy whose curly red hair gave a clue who his mother was. As far as he could tell, there were no photos of the boy's father.

She handed him the paperwork. "Look it over carefully."

Adam didn't need a microscope or a magnifying glass to see that the terms of the agreement favored the landlady. Big-time.

"I wasn't aware that this was the down payment on purchasing the property."

"A landlord needs some safeguards," she explained.

If she was a single mom, that would account for the financial safeguards stipulated in the agreement. "That's quite a hefty security deposit."

"But necessary."

"And this penalty for early lease termination seems excessive in addition to spelling out that a tenant is on the hook to pay the agreed-upon rent for the duration of the contract or until an alternative renter is secured."

"Also necessary," she said. "The costs of cleaning and painting between renters adds up. Then I have the costs of advertising to fill the vacancy on top of the lost revenue."

"But I'm not going to skip out on the rent."

"That's what they all say." Even if the tone hadn't given her away, skepticism was there in the expression on her face. "This covers the winter months. In spring and summer there's a better chance of getting a tenant who sticks."

"What makes you so sure I won't?"

"The last doctor took off after the first snow."

"I'm not the last doctor."

"Right," she said. "The clinic will replace you when you go."

"That's not what I meant and I'm pretty sure you know it."

"Doesn't make it any less true."

He leaned a hip against her desk. "Are you trying to talk me out of renting from you?"

"Is it working?" she asked, neither confirming nor denying the accusation.

"Correct me if I'm wrong, but real estate is business. It feels like you're making this personal."

"It's both. I already spelled out the business part in the contract." Her gaze rested on the photo he'd noticed moments ago. "I'm a single woman with a child. That gives me a personal interest in who lives upstairs. It's why I do a pretty thorough background screening before even showing the place to a prospective tenant. The town sheriff is a good friend of mine."

He guessed that she'd hoped to turn up something that would give her a reason to tell him no. As a businesswoman she needed to show the empty apartment to everyone who didn't have a black mark on their record. But he asked anyway. "Did I pass the test?"

Her smile seemed reluctant, but that didn't detract from its beauty. "I usually take families' testimonials with a grain of salt, but yours are different."

"I'm aware of that, but why do *you* think so?"

"When your dad is a Nobel Prize–winning economist and your mother a nationally known biomedical engineer, not to mention your brother is one of the country's top cardiac surgeons, that tends to carry some weight."

"You have no idea." The burden of being related to the gifted and geekish had finally worked in his favor.

"And you're a family practice doctor." There was a thoughtful expression on her face as she tucked a strand of curly red hair behind her ear. "Did your folks bring the wrong baby home from the hospital?"

"I get that a lot." Long ago he'd learned not to take it personally. His line of work was exactly what he wanted. "I'd probably have done a DNA test except I look like my dad and I have a twin sister."

"Is she a doctor, too?"

"Yeah. Rocket science. She works for NASA."

"Wow. Your family has some very impressive credentials," she commented.

"So you know my background. That doesn't explain your hard-line rental policy."

"If you think about it, it kind of does."

Adam looked at her. "How?"

"I have to wonder why you're here at all."

"I'm not sure I understand what you're asking." Actually he understood exactly what was on her mind.

He'd fielded lots of endless questions about his career and life choice, especially from the overachievers in his family. The perception was that he wasn't as good if this was the best medical specialty he could do. His ex-wife had no problem dumping him when he'd made the decision. It wasn't flashy enough for her and Adam was still bitter enough to make Jill say straight out what he knew she was thinking.

"Blackwater Lake is a small town."

"But growing," he pointed out.

"Yes." There was a sexy little dent in her chin that was more pronounced when her full lips were pulled tight. "But right now it's not very big. Summer is winding down and winter comes early in northern Montana. You could have your pick of warm places to practice medicine."

Someone, probably his mother, had shared information about offers he'd fielded from Los Angeles, San Francisco, Miami and Dallas, where he'd been working until recently.

Taking any one of them in a major metropolitan area would have gone a long way toward reassuring his family about what they considered his lack of ambition.

He'd accepted a long time ago that they would never understand why he wanted to treat the whole person, whole families, rather than be a world-renowned expert in a single body part. If the people who knew him best didn't get it, there was no way to explain it to a woman with a chip on her shoulder.

Adam decided to try anyway. "I found out early in medical school that factors beyond disease and diagnosis affect an individual's health. Treating the whole patient and not simply specializing in a certain organ of the body was important to me. Knowing the people in their world factors into the medical protocols. I like people."

"That's very noble of you." She sounded sincere and hopefully impressed. "But why here?"

"I came to a camp in Blackwater Lake. My parents were busy and gone a lot, so keeping us kids busy and out of trouble was important. I fell in love with this place and never forgot it. Being part of a community is important to me. So, when an opening came up in the clinic, I applied."

"I'm guessing you spent more than one summer here at camp?"

"Every one for nine years." He nodded emphatically. "Dallas is great, but big. Seeing the contrast between there and here convinced me that small-town life was just my cup of tea. I want to live and work here in Blackwater Lake."

"That's easy for you to say when the weather is beautiful, like it is today. But what about when you have to fight your way to the clinic through a blizzard?" She held up a hand when he opened his mouth to protest. "I can tell you what happens. You change your mind about small-town life. You run, not walk, to the closest airport and it's not all that close.

You get on a flight to the nearest big city and guess who's left holding the bag—or the lease. I have a family to support."

That sounded like confirmation that there was no ex helping her out with raising her son. Someone had obviously done her wrong, so he had to sign a legal contract to give her peace of mind.

Adam didn't react well to negative vibes, and Jill Beck had *N-O* with a capital *N* coming off her in waves. That made him want to challenge her and he could feel his stubborn streak going radioactive. It didn't always lead to the best personal decisions, and he had the only divorce in the family to prove the point. But the obstinate side always made his life interesting.

"I still want to rent your apartment, Miss Beck."

Her gaze narrowed on him. "You do realize what kind of money is involved?"

"In spite of my less challenging career choice, I did make it through medical school. I can do the math." He looked around at the living room with fresh flowers and more than one oval-framed needlepoint sampler. "This is charming. And the cost is not a problem."

"All right, Doctor—"

"If my personal check isn't satisfactory, I'd be happy to stop at the bank for cash or a cashier's check." He took a pen from her desk and signed the agreement. After handing it back he said, "You're going to be my landlady. It's time you started calling me Adam."

Adam.

Stone.

The name suited him, Jill thought. He was immovable like a rock. A tall, good-looking rock.

The man was her worst nightmare and he was settling in upstairs. The moving truck had brought his stuff and then rumbled away a while ago. On paper he was the perfect tenant. A doctor. Gainfully employed at Mercy Medical Clinic. He came from a prominent family. And the hefty check he'd given her had cleared the bank. Probably soared more than cleared. There was that prominent, wealthy family. But the doctor gig no doubt paid pretty well without help from the folks. That was the business part of her talking.

From Jill's personal perspective, he couldn't have been worse. Young. Too handsome for her own good. He reminded her of the actor who had played the most recent Captain James T. Kirk in *Star Trek*. She had a crush on that actor, and now his clone was living upstairs. Even worse, she liked him. He was funny and charming. Damn him.

None of that was even a problem—until he left. And he would. Like she'd told him, they all left. She should be used to men walking away from her by now, but apparently one never quite got the hang of having one's hopes crushed into dust. It still smarted. But she was a big girl and understood what was going on. Her son was just a little boy and she wouldn't stand by and allow a good-looking tenant to trample on C.J.'s feelings again.

Speaking of her son…

Jill pushed away from her desk and rubbed her eyes after looking at a computer screen for so long. This economics assignment for her online class had taken more time than anticipated. "C.J.?"

There was no answer and the house was too hushed and silent. He was a six-year-old boy, not a cat burglar, and quiet wasn't hardwired into him.

"C.J., are you hiding?" She stood, then listened for the giggling, a clue there was an unannounced game under way.

The only sounds came from overhead—faint footsteps and a thump. Doctor Dazzling was putting things away. Should she offer to help? Not if she was smart.

She walked down the hall to her son's room, which was where she'd last seen him, playing with action figures now abandoned on the beige area rug. His bed was made, the lumps and bumps in the superhero spread evidence of the small hands doing the big job. The boy attached to those hands was nowhere in sight.

"C.J.?" Jill opened the closet to make sure her mischievous little man wasn't playing with her.

The interior looked as if a clothing and toy store had thrown up. When he was ordered to put his stuff away, this was where C.J. stashed everything. But if he were hiding in here, there would be giggling and wiggling. His skill level for holding still was on a par with keeping quiet.

Now she was starting to get concerned. He couldn't maintain the cone of silence for very long, but sneaking out of the house without being heard was something he was pretty good at. If he'd left the premises, she knew where to find him.

She walked over to her desk, picked up the phone and hit speed dial. It rang several times before the man who worked her marina business on the lake answered. "Blackwater Lake Marina and Bait Shop."

"Brewster? It's Jill."

"Hey, boss. What's up?"

"Tell C.J. it's time for him to come home. And he's in big trouble." She half sat on the edge of her desk.

"I'd be happy to except he's not here."

Her stomach knotted with worry. "Are you sure? Maybe he sneaked in quietly. You know how he loves to jump out and scare you."

"That's a fact. But I've been out front all afternoon straightening up. No way he could get by me."

"Okay. Thanks."

"You want me to look for him?"

"No. I'm sure he's in the house somewhere. Bye, Brew."

No need to panic. This was probably a new unannounced game, something he did frequently. But from the moment he was born she'd used all her senses to keep tabs on her little guy, and sight was the one that brought her the most comfort. Seeing him safe and sound always made her breathe a sigh of relief. She badly wanted that sigh now.

Overhead she heard more footsteps followed by another thump. Her eyes narrowed as a thought formed. "He wouldn't dare—"

Jill walked out her front door and turned right, then went up the stairs and knocked on her new tenant's door. Moments later he opened it and smiled. Her stomach boomeranged down to her toes and back up. It had happened the first time she saw him, but she'd been sure the reaction was a one-time deal and was now under control. Apparently it needed some more work.

"Hi," he said. "What's up? Do you need more money?"

"Not until next month." In spite of the niggling guilt she smiled. Might as well be friendly. No way she could avoid dealing with him. "Are you settling in okay?"

"Yeah. Thanks for asking." His gaze sharpened a fraction as he studied her. "Is something wrong?"

Jill figured either he was superobservant, or she should never try to improve her financial situation by playing poker.

"Actually," she said, "I was wondering if you'd seen my son."

"Is he about this high?" Adam put his hand about C.J.'s height. "Curly red hair? Wearing jeans, sneakers and a Spider-Man T-shirt? Looks a lot like you."

"A perfect description. That means you've spotted him recently." The knot of anxiety in her stomach loosened.

"Yeah. He's been helping me put things away."

"You should have sent him home." The anxiety snapped

back, but for a different reason. "He knows better than to pester our renter."

Adam folded his arms over his chest. There was something so blatantly masculine in the movement that her mouth went dry. Until that moment, Jill hadn't considered how long it had been since her last date. Apparently too long. Might be time to do something about that.

"By 'knows better,' do you mean he had specific instructions not to come upstairs?"

She nodded. "The exact words were that there would be dire consequences if he bothered you."

"Then he's off the hook."

"How do you figure?" she asked.

"Because he's not bothering me."

Adam Stone was covering for C.J., she realized. It was protective and sweet. Unfortunately, she couldn't afford to give in to that "aww" feeling. It would open the door for the "oh, damn" feeling when he left. She was the only one C.J. could count on. It was *her* job to protect him.

The sound of small sneakers running sounded just before the little guy appeared beside the big guy. "Hi, Mom. I didn't sneak out and help Brew at the dock because I had to help Adam."

There were so many things wrong with that statement she didn't know where to start, but he was gone before she could say anything. And that was classic C.J. They needed to have a conversation, but before that she needed to set boundaries with Adam. When she did, it would be best if her son was out of earshot.

"He didn't tell me where he was going," she started.

"You were worried."

"Of course." It was probably an educated guess, because her background check confirmed he was a bachelor without children. He had no frame of reference to empathize with a parent.

"I should have asked if he had permission." There was annoyance in his expression that looked to be self-directed. "It won't happen again. You have my word."

"That's very much appreciated," she said sincerely. "But here's the thing. Probably it's better for C.J. if you don't encourage him to hang out with you at all."

Adam leaned a broad shoulder against the doorjamb. "Are you telling me to stay away from him?"

"No. Not exactly." Unable to meet his gaze, she looked down at the wood floor on the landing outside his door. "Kind of."

"I expect you've got a good reason." The deep tone dripping with sarcasm said he didn't believe there was such a thing.

"I'm a single parent—"

"So you said."

"And C.J. is an active, outgoing little boy."

That made him smile. "He's a really great kid."

"I know." She smiled, too. Then grew serious. "He's a great kid who badly wants a man in his life to hang out with."

"Just my opinion as a family practice doctor, but that's perfectly normal."

"It's probably not a good idea for him to get attached to you." She met his gaze. "That's just my opinion as his mother."

"Because you think I won't stick."

"Exactly. I just don't want him to get his little heart broken again—" A lump of emotion lodged in her throat and it was mortifying in front of this man.

"The last doctor," he guessed.

His parents and siblings weren't the only smart ones in

the Stone family. She was trying to be vague, but apparently he had a gift for connecting the dots. "Yeah."

"I wouldn't hurt him, Jill." The tone was extraordinarily gentle.

"Not deliberately," she said. "I know that. But it concerns me."

"I admire your impulse to protect him and will do my best to help you out."

Jill hadn't realized she was spoiling for a fight until he didn't give her one. She appreciated the compliment about her maternal instincts, and the admiration went both ways. He seemed like a good guy, but another seemingly good guy had once stood right where he was now. That guy broke his promise and her son's heart. Jill's had been nicked, too.

"Thanks for understanding." What else could she say?

"I'm still not going anywhere." Before that could be challenged, he called out, "C.J.? Your mom says it's time to go home."

"Do I have to?" The question was followed by the *tap, tap* of running sneakers. The boy stopped beside Adam. "My tummy isn't tellin' me it's time for dinner yet, Mom."

"It's still time to go home," she said firmly, noting the way Adam's mouth twitched as he struggled not to laugh.

"Why?" the boy asked.

"Because you've bothered Adam enough for one day."

"I didn't bother him. Did I?" C.J. looked up, the beginnings of hero worship on his freckled face.

Adam glanced at her, caught between a rock and a hard place. Then he answered without actually answering. "Your mom has her reasons. If I were you, I'd do what she says."

"Okay." Then a thought chased away his disappointment. "Can Adam have dinner with us?"

"It's Dr. Stone," she corrected the little boy.

"He said to call him Adam," C.J. protested.

"I did," he confirmed. "You could take lessons."

"Right." Jill smiled. "How about a compromise, kiddo? What do you think of Dr. Adam?"

"I think he's cool," C.J. answered.

"I meant that's what you should call him. Remember, respect for your elders."

"Moving day is always tough," Adam said, "but I didn't feel quite so old until just now."

"Can Dr. Adam have dinner with us?" the relentless child persisted.

"I don't think so, kiddo." She looked at Dr. Adam, and there must have been pleading in her eyes.

"Not tonight, buddy." Adam's expression was half amused, half regretful. "I still have a lot of boxes to unpack."

Jill appreciated his cooperation and knew what was coming from her son. "No, you can't help, C.J."

"Aw, Mom—" Hope filled his brown eyes. "What about when he's done unpacking? He might get lonesome."

"You're pushing it, mister. Downstairs. On the double." She glanced over her shoulder and thought Dr. Adam might have been looking at her butt.

It was a nice thought, but a waste of his time and energy. A crush on the movie star type notwithstanding, she would never let Adam Stone be her type.

Jill walked C.J. down the stairs and when they got to the bottom she saw Brewster Smith walking up the path. He stopped in front of her, on the covered porch.

"Just came by to see if you found C.J." The man was in his fifties and had a full head of gray hair and a beard to match. Very mountain-man-looking. He was an employee, but more important, her friend. "I see you did."

"Yes, he was—"

"Hey, Brew," C.J. said. "I was helpin' Dr. Adam unpack

his stuff and he's got a lot! Mostly books. Really big, fat ones. He said they're too heavy for me."

Jill put a hand on her son's small shoulder. "I'm sorry if I worried you, Brew. He neglected to tell me where he was going."

"Figured that." The man's pale blue eyes narrowed. "If he had, you'd have put a stop to it."

This man knew her better than anyone, knew how hard it had been when she'd been left behind by the doctor. He was the one who'd held her when she cried.

The door at the top of the stairs opened and heavy footsteps sounded on the wood tread behind them. There was only one person it could be.

"C.J.? You forgot these." Adam handed over Batman and Captain America action figures. He nodded at Brew. "Hi."

The older man's eyes narrowed on the new guy in town. "You're the renter."

"Yeah." He held out his hand. "Adam Stone."

"Brewster Smith," he answered, taking the offered hand. "Nice to meet you."

"Hope you still think that when I say what's on my mind."

"Okay. Shoot."

"This woman is like a daughter to me." Brewster's face was all warning, no warmth. "Treat her right or I won't be a happy man."

"You're already not happy," Adam pointed out cheerfully, apparently not intimidated at all.

"If you do anything to hurt her, I'll be a whole lot not happier. And that goes for a lot of folks in town, too." The older man's gaze never wavered, before he abruptly turned and walked down the front porch steps. At the bottom he headed in the direction of the marina.

"Nice guy," Adam said. "Straightforward."

"He's a good friend."

Jill was grateful for his friendship and something else, too. The town was circling the wagons around her. It wasn't the first time this had happened, but it still made her very happy. In the case of Dr. Adam Stone it made her incredibly grateful. He'd done nothing to anesthetize her attraction and she'd need all the protection those circled wagons could give her.

Chapter Two

Adam had just seen his last patient on his first day at the clinic. He wouldn't say this was the worst day he'd ever had as a doctor, but moving from Texas and unpacking boxes had been a piece of cake compared to cutting through the glacial attitude of the people he'd seen today. Of course none of those people had been C. J. Beck, who couldn't have been cuter or friendlier, unlike his mom. Except for the cute part. Jill was more than cute. And that was nothing more than a guy's appreciative take on a very pretty, very sexy woman.

The surroundings were different from any office he'd ever worked in. Mercy Medical Clinic was set up in a large Victorian house that had been donated to the town years ago. The kitchen had been turned into an outpatient lab and the spacious living room now had sofas, chairs and tables for a waiting area. Bedrooms had been converted to exam rooms, and closets held medical and office supplies. That morning he'd had the two-cent tour from nurse Virginia Irvin, who was no warmer than the patients he'd seen. She was like a glacier in scrubs.

He grabbed a cup of coffee from the break area in the small alcove near the back door that was once a mudroom, then went back down the long hallway, past the exam rooms and to his office. It was time to catch up on paperwork.

So as not to keep patients waiting too long, there hadn't been time to do more than look at the updated medical information form he'd asked each patient to fill out and skim the chart for drug allergies. Now he wanted to look at all the information on each person he'd seen, including notes from the physicians who'd come before him. Including "the last doctor."

Those words worked on his nerves like something in his eye that wouldn't come out. Everyone he'd seen today had said it and in exactly the tone Jill used, the one that put him in the same slimy subspecies as the physician who'd run out on her and the rest of the town.

"There you are, Doctor."

He looked up from the stack of charts on his desk. Mercy Medical Clinic's nurse stood in the doorway. "Hi, Ginny."

"It's Virginia."

Apparently only to him, because everyone who wasn't gum on the bottom of her shoe called her Ginny. Somewhere in her late fifties or early sixties, she had silver hair cut in a pixie, blue eyes that missed nothing and no filter between her brain and her mouth. At least one knew where one stood with her. In his case, he was pretty sure she wished he was standing in Alaska. She was short on stature and long on attitude.

"Can I ask you something, Virginia?"

"Thought doctors knew everything. Like God." She folded her arms over her chest, and the body language felt like a *yes* to his question, so he continued.

"We just pretend to know everything. It makes the patients feel better." Maybe self-deprecation would thaw her out.

"Uh-huh."

Maybe not so much. "As a boy I spent a lot of summers here in Blackwater Lake and folks seemed a lot friendlier."

She looked down at him. "We're not in the habit of being mean to kids, especially ones who are visiting."

"So the friendly pill wears off when that kid grows up and moves here?"

"Something like that."

He was the new guy and she knew this clinic and everyone who used it inside and out, by all accounts an excellent nurse who would be difficult to replace. So he hid his frustration when he asked, "Can you be more specific?"

The gaze she leveled at him could laser a person's heart out. "It would help if you looked less like the good-looking actor in that space movie and more like Quasimodo."

Huh? There was a compliment in there somewhere, but he'd need a scalpel to remove it. "I'm not sure what you mean by that."

"Then I'll explain." She moved farther into the room. "If you were ugly as a mud fence and didn't rent a place from Jill Beck, folks here in town would give you the benefit of the doubt. But that's not the case. The last doctor—"

"Didn't stick," he interrupted. "Jill mentioned that."

"She's one of ours," the nurse continued. "Her mother was my best friend since third grade. The last thing I said to Dottie before she died was that I'd watch out for her little girl and her grandson."

Adam remembered what Brewster had said and figured Virginia and the patients he'd seen today were some of the folks who'd be a whole lot not happy if Jill got hurt.

"What happened to her mom?" he asked.

"Breast cancer." The woman's mouth pulled tight as if her lips would tremble without the control.

"I'm sorry."

"Me, too."

"The thing is, you don't need to protect Jill from me," Adam assured her.

"Uh-huh."

The sarcastic tone said there was nothing he could say to convince her, so he wasn't going to waste his breath trying. "Did you want something?" At her blank look, he added, "You were looking for me?"

"Right." The puzzled expression disappeared. "You've got one more patient. Little boy with a fever and sore throat. His daddy sweet-talked Liz into letting him come by."

Liz Carpenter was the clinic receptionist, a pretty young woman who apparently didn't need protecting from the big, bad outsider.

"Is he here?" Adam asked.

"Exam room one," the nurse answered.

"I'll be right there."

"He's ready for you." She turned and left his office.

It had been a warm, September day in Blackwater Lake, Montana, but Adam felt like digging out his winter parka before seeing the patient. He left his office and walked back down the hall. Exam one was the farthest away and the others were empty, so it wasn't hard to do the math. New doctor hazing, with a generous dose of warning tossed in.

He pulled the chart from the plastic holder on the wall beside the door and read the patient's name. Tyler Dixon. The last name was familiar.

Before going in he read the medical information. Tyler was six, about the same age as C. J. Beck. Not allergic to anything. An otherwise healthy boy with a sore throat and fever. His father was Cabot Dixon, and Adam grinned as he walked inside.

The dark-haired, dark-eyed little guy sitting on the exam table looked exactly like the boy his father had been when Adam had met him years ago. The Dixons owned the ranch where he'd gone to camp every summer and the two had become friends.

He held out his hand. "Cab, it's good to see you again."

"Adam." The other man's smile was sincere and friendly, a first for the day. "Heard you moved here, but didn't think I'd have to see you in a professional way so soon."

"Your boy's not feeling well?"

"This is Tyler."

"I didn't wanna miss school, but my froat hurts," the child informed him. "And I don't like shots."

"Me either." Adam smiled as he studied the boy's feverish eyes and flushed cheeks. "Would it be okay if I just take a peek in your throat?"

"Just look?" The boy didn't trust him, but that had nothing to do with Jill Beck and everything to do with being six years old.

"I want to feel your neck, too, but it won't hurt."

"Promise?"

Adam crossed his heart and held up his palm. "Word of honor."

"Okay."

Beside the exam table on a metal tray, nurse Virginia had put out some things. He picked up the wooden tongue blade and the handheld light and told Tyler to say "ah." Then he ran his fingers over the boy's neck and asked the father, "Has he had a cough or runny nose?"

"No."

Adam took the stethoscope from around his neck and listened to the small chest and back. "Strong heartbeat. Good bilateral breath sounds. No wheezing from upper or lower lobes of the lungs," he said.

"What is it, Adam?"

"My guess is strep throat. It usually shows up late fall to spring, so this is early, but symptoms are classic, including yellow patches on the back of his throat. I'll swab it and we can do a rapid strep test to confirm."

After Cabot nodded approval, Adam promised the little guy a "good boy" toy, then rubbed a cotton swab in the back of his throat. When Virginia came into the room he asked her to do the test on the sample and Tyler went with her to pick out his reward. That gave Adam a chance to talk to the man who'd befriended him when they were boys.

"Don't worry, Cab. It's not serious. Strep usually goes away without treatment and only rarely turns into something more serious. I'll give you a prescription for an antibiotic, but it's just a precaution."

"That's a relief." The rugged man clearly had a soft spot where his son was concerned, and that was as it should be. "Anything else I should do?"

"Make sure Ty gets over-the-counter meds for the fever and lots of fluids—soda in moderation, popsicles, juice and water." But Adam wondered about Cabot's wife. It was most often the mother who came in with a sick child. "So, when did you get married?"

"Six years, eight months ago." There was no mistaking the anger that slid, hot and intense, into those dark eyes. "And I got divorced right after Ty was born because she walked out. Left me with an infant and no idea how to take care of him. Still, he's the best thing she gave me and I have to thank her for him. Just an FYI, don't bring a city girl to Blackwater Lake. If you want to be happy for the rest of your life, make a local girl your wife."

"Had a wife once," Adam said. "Don't want another one, thanks."

"Want to talk about it?"

"No. You?"

"No." His friend smiled. "So, how's Blackwater Lake treating you?"

"Like a leper," he admitted.

"I heard you rented Jill Beck's apartment."

"Guilty. And apparently that's a hanging offense as far as people in this town are concerned, because I haven't even screwed up yet."

Cabot shrugged. "You're paying the price for the doctor who rented her place and then charmed and harmed her. Folks don't like it when an outsider dumps on one of their own."

"She's safe from me," Adam protested. "I just want to be part of the community. End of story. Honest."

"I believe you." The other man's expression was amused and sympathetic. "But you'll never belong until you prove you're not going to 'do Jill wrong.'"

"Tell me how to convince folks and I'll do it." Adam figured he'd take all the help he could get, especially from someone who knew the locals.

"You're on your own with that."

Before he could say more, Tyler came back into the room to show off his toy car and Adam was no closer to solving his problem. He liked Jill. He was attracted to her, but starting something was problematic. A single mom in Blackwater Lake would want promises and vows, and that was something he'd never do again.

To start anything he had no intention of following through on would make him no better than the last doctor, which would only drive the wedge deeper between him and the community. He didn't get through medical school being stupid, so somehow he'd find a way to live under her roof and not complicate the situation by getting personal.

The best approach was to take the advice he so often gave his patients. Give it time. Unfortunately, he *wasn't* patient.

Potter's Ice Cream Parlor wasn't busy on a weeknight now that the kids had returned to school from summer vacation. Jill was filling in for her friend Maggie and it was kind of a relief to be here as opposed to her own house where she couldn't stop thinking about Adam Stone and the fact that only a ceiling separated them. Glancing at the display case, she made sure none of the ice cream flavors needed a refill. Beside it, all the sundae toppings, including nuts, crushed candy and fruit, were all full.

In front of the counter, all the cute little chairs with heart-shaped backs were tucked neatly under circular tables. The walls were filled with brightly colored prints of candy sprinkles, nuts and cherries. Right behind the cash register was a photo of Maggie Potter and her husband, Dan, in his Army National Guard uniform, hugging and happy on the day they'd opened this place a couple of years ago. Now her husband was dead and Maggie was dealing with everything by herself. Jill was going to help as best she could.

There wasn't much to do, so she grabbed a damp rag and started to wipe down the stainless-steel counters. With her back to the front door she relied on the old-fashioned bell above it to alert her to a customer. When it rang she turned to see who was there.

"Hey, you two." She smiled at Norm and Diane Schurr, friends of her mom. He was about six feet five and thin, with white hair. His blonde wife was about a foot shorter and always watching her weight. "What'll you have?"

"Three scoops of vanilla in a cup with caramel and nuts," Norm said.

Like the retired school teacher she was, Diane gave him a stern look. "You're supposed to be watching your cholesterol."

"Okay, then," her husband said good-naturedly, "make it two scoops."

"Oh, for goodness' sake." His wife laughed and shook her head. "I'll have the nonfat cookies 'n' cream yogurt—a small."

"Coming right up." While Jill worked on filling their order she asked, "What's new?"

"Not much with us, but Brewster Smith says you filled your vacancy. Mercy Medical Clinic's new doctor." Diane's gaze was full of warning.

"It's true." Gosh darn it.

"The doctor is very good-looking," the woman added.

"You've met him?" Jill handed over Norm's sundae above the high glass of the display case.

"Had an appointment today for my checkup," he answered.

"We both did," his wife said. "The thing is, sweetheart, you shouldn't let a pretty face tempt you into letting your guard down again."

"Don't worry." She turned to the yogurt dispenser and depressed the handle to let the creamy stuff make a volcano-shaped mound in the cup. "Even if I weakened, I know I can count on good friends like you to pull me back from the edge."

"Darn right," Norm said.

"That'll be seven dollars and three cents," she said.

Norm put down his cup and reached for his wallet. "It's too bad."

"I know, but Maggie wouldn't make any money if the order was free," Jill teased.

"Not that," he said, waving away her words with a twenty-dollar bill in his hand. "It's a shame you can't go after the doc. He seems like a real nice young man."

So did the last doctor, until he left. *Fool me once, shame on you. Fool me twice, shame on me,* Jill thought.

After handing over change, she said, "So, how did your appointment go? You guys doing okay?"

"Pretty good," the man answered. "I'm not gettin' any younger, but I got a strong body. Doc said it's like a muscle car. If you put junk in the tank, you're gonna get a junk performance."

"So you have three scoops of ice cream," his wife said wryly.

"Only two, dear." His blue eyes twinkled with mischief. "Dr. Stone told us we have the time to take care of ourselves because we're retired. We want to enjoy it."

"Of course you do." Who wouldn't? Jill thought. She just couldn't imagine leisure time for herself. Ever.

There were bills to pay and a son to raise, plus a little bit to put away for the college fund he would need someday. She barely scraped by now and only had herself to depend on. The idea of not working was a luxury she couldn't even think about. "But you guys are okay?"

Diane nodded. "The doctor says we're both healthy, but to watch our cholesterol and blood pressure."

"So Dr. Stone didn't tell you anything you didn't already know?" Jill asked.

"No. But he spent a lot of time doing it, not like the one who always rushed us in and out. Dr. Stone said our hearts are strong. Walking is a good exercise and he couldn't think of a more beautiful place than Blackwater Lake to do it in. Clean air. Majestic mountains. Trees. Said a person could exercise body and soul at the same time."

The bell over the door jangled and in walked the doctor/poet himself. Jill wondered if her own heart was strong enough to survive the pounding it took every time she saw him, and now was no exception. The Schurrs looked like twin deer caught in headlights. Or kids with their hands in the cookie jar.

"Dr. Stone," Diane said. "Speaking of the devil. We didn't expect to see you here."

"Besides being the devil," he said with a straight face and a gleam of amusement in his eyes, "I'm also the food police."

"This is yogurt." The older woman's voice was only a little bit defensive. "Ask Jill."

Apparently Adam hadn't noticed her behind the tall glass case, because he looked surprised. "So you're the witness for the defense?"

"Mrs. Schurr is telling the whole truth and nothing but." She couldn't stop a smile. "And as chief of the food police, you should deputize her. She cut Mr. Schurr back from three scoops to two."

The doctor nodded. "Have you thought about coming out of retirement and taking on a new career in diplomatic negotiations? You'd be good at it."

"I should be after all those years in the classroom. Girls and boys need a firm hand and the voice of reason." She finished the last of her yogurt and looked at Jill. "Norm and I have to be going. It's good to see you, sweetheart. Take good care."

"Will do," Jill answered, reading the real meaning between the lines. "Night, Mrs. Schurr. Mr. Schurr."

The two waved, and then the bell above the door jangled before they walked out and she was alone with Adam. He was wearing worn jeans and a black T-shirt that snugly covered his broad chest like a second skin. The sleeves stretched over his biceps and drew her attention to the contour of muscle there. The devil impressed her female hormones, she thought.

And it was okay to be impressed as long as that didn't blind her to reality.

"So, you didn't really come in here to be the food police, did you? That could put a big dent in Maggie's income. She does a lot of business with the town's retired demographic."

"No, I'm not checking up." He laughed. "I have a confession to make, though."

Being married, having a girlfriend and leaving tomorrow were the top three declarations of guilt that popped into Jill's mind. But all she said was, "Oh? What?"

"I can't say no to ice cream."

"Neither can my son, which I guess makes me the food police."

"Good luck with that. C.J. is resourceful and could join Mrs. Schurr in diplomatic negotiations."

"Or undiplomatic," she added. "What can I get you?"

"I'll have what Mr. Schurr had." Adam folded his arms over his chest and studied her as if she were a new and exotic flavor in the display case.

She scooped the ice cream into a cup, then took the ladle to drizzle caramel over the two vanilla mounds. She was grateful to have something to do with her hands and very aware that his gaze never left her. "Is something wrong?"

"You tell me." He took the cup she handed him. "Where's C.J.? And what are you doing here?"

"My son is with Brewster and his wife, Hildie." Not that it was any of his business. "And I'm here because Maggie Potter is pregnant and having contractions. Her brother drove her to the hospital."

"The closest one is over seventy miles away. And she's only seven months along."

"How do you know that?"

A wry expression chased away the concern for a moment. "This isn't my first time here in the parlor."

"Right. Ice cream obsession." She nodded.

He moved to the lower counter where the cash register was located and braced a hip against it as he ate. "Why did her brother take her? Where's her husband?"

"He was in the army. Killed in Afghanistan. She found out not long ago." And obviously hadn't shared the information with a stranger, even if he was a doctor and a regular customer.

"Damn it. I don't even know what to say. That…" Adam jammed his plastic spoon into the ice cream and set it down. He shook his head and the sympathy in his eyes was wrapped in an anger that looked sincere. "It just sucks."

"I know."

"The shock could have brought on early labor," he said.

"I hope not. Baby's still small."

"She's pretty upset," Jill confirmed.

"So you're filling in."

"It's the least I can do," she said. "Maggie and Dan built this business from scratch. I've known them both since we were all in kindergarten together. They were high school sweethearts. He was the love of her life and my good friend. No one can bring him back, but if there's anything I can do to save his child, I'll do it. And keeping this place alive is as much for him as for Maggie."

"It's a wonderful gesture."

There was a hint of surprise in his voice that Jill resented. Or maybe she just took exception to him, however unfair that was. Or it could be her reaction was more about looking for a reason to keep up a robust level of mad to squash or squeeze out the stubborn attraction to him that she couldn't seem to shake.

Whatever her motivation, there was an edge to her voice when she said, "Friends are *there* for each other."

"I couldn't agree more." His voice had an edge, too, and

the words clearly indicated he hadn't missed the underlying meaning in her words. There was a spark of anger in his blue eyes that had nothing to do with loss from a war halfway around the world and everything to do with conflict between the two of them. "And I'll look forward to someone being there for me when I have more than one friend in town."

"You actually have one now?" she asked, leaning a hip on the other side of the counter.

"As a matter of fact, I do. Cabot Dixon and I go way back to my summer camp days. His father's ranch is where my parents sent me, and we hit it off."

"C.J. and Tyler are good buddies," she said.

"I wondered. Cab brought the boy in and I noticed that he's the same age."

"Hope it was nothing serious."

"No." Adam shook his head. "But because of patient privacy laws I can't say more than that."

"Don't break any rules on my account."

"Not to worry. But there is something I plan to do on your account."

"Don't do me any favors."

"Actually it's me I'm concerned about." He picked up his ice cream again and started eating. "It seems the people here in town are all very protective of you. To win their hearts and minds I need to prove myself to you, earn your friendship. And that's exactly what I intend to do."

"Good luck with that." She struggled for a flip attitude but was pretty sure it didn't work, what with her heart pounding so hard. "I've built up an immunity to nice, charming men."

"Then it's a good thing I'm not nice or charming." He finished the last of his sundae and dropped the cup and spoon in the trash.

Suddenly Jill realized he hadn't paid for it. "I forgot to

ring up that ice cream. Some friend I am. That's no way to mind Maggie's store."

He reached into his jeans pocket and slid out some folded bills. After pulling one from the wad, he put it on the counter and said, "Keep the change." Then he met her gaze and said, "Jill?"

She couldn't look away even if she wanted to. "What?"

"I'm really not the devil."

She'd have to take his word on that because right now she was pretty sure he was. He tempted her just by walking in and breathing the same air. Technically he lived right above her and probably they were trading oxygen and carbon monoxide all night long. That could do a number on her if she thought about it too long.

So she wouldn't think about it, and no way was friendship a possibility. Men and women couldn't be friends. More often than not, it went bad. She didn't need any more bad in her life than she'd already had.

Chapter Three

It was Saturday and Adam didn't know what to do with his first real weekend off since moving to Blackwater Lake. He wandered around the apartment that grew on him more every day. The boxes were gone, stuff was put away and pictures were hung. They weren't as soul-stunning as Jill's, but he planned to take his own photos and get some shots that were wall-worthy.

His computer was hooked up and on the desk in the second bedroom he was using as a home office. Medical books and a few fiction paperbacks were stacked on the floor, and he could use some bookcases. A trip to the antiques and furniture stores in town could fill some time today.

Then he looked out the living room window with a view of the lake. There was a small wooden building nearby with a sign that read Blackwater Lake Marina and Bait Shop. It was about time he explored his new hometown, starting with what was right in his own backyard.

He grabbed his keys, locked the front door, then jogged down the stairs to the covered porch. Beside Jill's door sat a pair of C.J.-sized muddy sneakers and a small baseball mitt. Just a guess but both probably belonged to the little guy who lived downstairs. Thoughts of the redheaded rascal made him smile and he wondered what the kid was up to on a day off from school. Hopefully hanging out with Tyler Dixon on the ranch where a kid could be a kid. Adam wouldn't trade his time there for anything. And what C.J. did was none of his business since his redheaded, red-hot mom had warned him off.

He walked down the path and turned right, heading for the marina store. A few minutes later he stepped onto the wooden walkway outside. A few yards from the door, the dock jutted into the lake, a small number of boats tied up on either side.

He entered the store and waited for his eyes to adjust from the bright sunshine outside. Bending over a box, Jill had her back to the door and was restocking the tall, refrigerated case with bottled water. Before she straightened he had time to look his fill and conclude that she did have one terrific tush.

And that kind of thinking was to his goal what the iceberg was to the *Titanic*. To win over the people of Blackwater Lake, he had to be her friend, nothing more.

"Mom?" That was C.J.'s voice.

Adam moved a step farther inside and saw the kid. Racks of souvenir T-shirts had hidden him, sitting cross-legged on the floor beside the cold case. His elbows were resting on his knees, and his small, freckled face was cradled in both hands. If he was a photo, Adam would title it *Boredom*.

"Mom," he said again, louder this time.

"What, kiddo?"

"Why can't I go outside?"

"Because you're not allowed to play by the lake when there's no one to watch you. That's the rule."

"It's a stupid rule. I know how to swim."

"True. But better safe than sorry," she said.

"I'm already sorry because I can't go outside."

Adam smothered a laugh. This kid was priceless.

"I wanna go to Ty's house," he said, taking a new direction.

"We've been through this already. I have to mind the store, so I can't drive you."

"I could call Ty. I bet Mr. Dixon could come and get me, Mom."

"He's busy running his ranch. You shouldn't bother him," she said.

"When's Brew coming back?"

"A couple of hours."

The kid let out a big sigh. "I don't got nothin' to do for a couple hours."

"I don't have anything to do," she corrected.

"Then you can drive me to Ty's."

Adam cleared his throat to cover a laugh and let them know he was standing there. "Hi."

"Dr. Adam!" C.J. jumped up and ran over.

"Hi, champ." He made a fist and the kid did the same and bumped it. Looking at Jill, he said, "Good morning."

"How are you?" She brushed the curly red hair off her forehead.

"Good. Enjoying a day off."

"Must be nice," she said wistfully.

"It is."

He saw the dark circles under her eyes and asked, "Is there any place in town you don't work?"

She laughed, which was a nice surprise. "Potter's Parlor was for Maggie, but this store is mine."

"Interesting place," he said, glancing around.

Fishing poles were standing along one wooden wall, and

above them was a divided case with lures, sinkers and bait. Another wall had cubbyholes holding hats, and beside it were stacks of ice chests. In the center space were racks of outdoor clothing—quilted vests, flannel shirts, windbreakers and light jackets.

"Brewster works for me, so I take over when he's off."

"Who takes over when you're off?"

"It's not an issue."

The subtext was that she never had time off. But there wasn't any trace of self-pity in her tone or expression. All he saw was strength and pride. The combination made her stunning, the kind of woman he wanted to get to know better.

He started to say something but was interrupted by the sound of heavy footsteps on the wooden walkway outside just before three men came into the store. They were all about the same age, in their late fifties or early sixties.

Jill smiled. "Welcome to Blackwater Lake."

Adam listened to the conversation and figured out that these guys were strangers to her, new to the area and looking for fishing gear. Jill led them to the wall with rods and reels, then began answering their questions regarding the pros and cons of each type and its relation to their skill level.

While she was preoccupied with customers and a potentially lucrative sale, her son slipped outside, unnoticed by anyone but Adam. He stood in the store's doorway and saw C.J. race down to the lake's edge, then bend to grab a rock and throw it into the water. So much for mom's rule. And Jill was right to worry about safety around the water.

Adam walked down the path and stopped beside the boy. He picked up a smooth stone, then flicked his wrist and watched it skip three times before disappearing.

"Cool," C.J. said. "How did you learn to do that?"

"Tyler's dad showed me when I was just about your age."

The boy looked up, squinting into the sun. "Did you live here then?"

"I only visited during the summer."

"Are you and Mr. Dixon friends?"

"Yes." So far the only one he had in Blackwater Lake. As far as Jill was concerned, C.J. didn't count.

"Can you teach me how to skip rocks?" he asked eagerly.

"I can show you. Then it's just practice to get the hang of it."

"Forget it, then. I'll never get good." C.J. kicked at the rocky shore with the toe of a sneaker. "I'm not s'posed to be here alone. But Mom never has time to watch me."

"She has a lot of responsibility." He could relate. Jill was a single mom, but Adam had two parents, and their demanding careers had left little time to spend with a boy who wanted to play. He'd been turned over to others to be supervised, then spent summers here. As an adult he understood, but thank goodness for those summers. "But I'm here now."

"You can watch me?"

"Yeah." He picked up another stone and demonstrated the proper way to hold it, between thumb and forefinger. "It's all in the wrist."

C.J. watched as he threw it and said, "Let me try."

They worked on the skill for five minutes, which is about all the attention span a six-year-old has. After that the boy used the rocks like a depth charge, aiming for the fish darting around just below the surface.

"I'm a mighty hunter," he said, moving so close the water almost lapped over his shoe.

Adam was ready to grab him if there was a chance he'd fall in. "Do you have a fishing pole?"

"Not yet. Mom says when I'm seven."

"When's that?"

"When it gets cold."

He remembered Jill telling him that the doctor had left as soon as it turned cold. Had he been there for the kid's birthday or skipped out before? She'd said she wouldn't allow her son's heart to be broken *again,* which meant he'd already been hurt once. That sucked.

"Does it hurt the fish when you hook 'em?"

Probably, Adam thought. But he didn't want to tell the boy that. The crunch of footsteps behind them saved him from having to answer, but the look on Jill's face told him he wasn't saved from anything else.

"Uh-oh," C.J. said. "It's my mom."

Uh-oh, indeed.

"I'm very disappointed in you, C.J."

Adam knew from personal experience that the disappointment card was the biggest gun in the parental arsenal. But a safety rule had been broken.

"Are you mad, Mom?"

"Do I look mad?" Her voice was deadly quiet and calm. Shouting would have been easier to take.

C.J. studied her expression. "No?" he asked hopefully.

She shook her head. "You disobeyed a direct order right after we talked about it."

Adam looked from her to C.J., knowing she'd just taken the "I forgot" defense out of play.

"There has to be consequences, kiddo."

"Am I grounded?"

"I have to think about this," she said.

"While you're thinkin'," he said, rubbing a finger along the side of his nose, "remember Ty's birthday party is in a week."

"Thank you for reminding me," she said.

It was that quiet voice that finally got to Adam. He couldn't just stand there and say nothing. "Look, Jill, it's Saturday and the sun is out. Awfully tough for a guy to be cooped up indoors. I was here—"

"About that," she said, her tone edging up. She looked at her son. "Run up to the store and get a drink of water, C.J. I need to talk to Adam."

For just a second he teetered on the verge of argument, then just nodded. Without a word he trudged back up the path and disappeared through the door to the marina store.

"Jill, don't take it out on him. I'm the one you're really mad at."

Her brown eyes darkened with anger. "I made it clear that letting him get attached to you isn't an option. Water safety isn't the only issue here. It's my job to look out for him emotionally, too."

"And I made it clear that I wouldn't hurt him."

"Talk is cheap." The breeze blew a strand of hair across her eyes and she angrily brushed it away.

"I was just keeping him company—in the spirit of helping someone out," he said.

"I don't need that kind of help. When he gets attached to you and is left behind—"

"I'm going to be a part of this community where people look out for one another." He hadn't planned to defend himself, but hearing about the last doctor was getting old. "Blackwater Lake is a place where neighbors pitch in. It's what you did for Maggie. That's all I was doing with C.J."

"*I* look out for him," she said.

"So you can be there for a friend, but I can't? Smacks of a double standard to me."

"That's because you're not a single mom." She nodded for emphasis, then turned away and walked back up the path after her son.

Adam watched her stiff back and not for the first time he thought she had a little too much spine. Bending a little would do her good, and he was just the guy who could outstubborn her.

That's when it hit him that instead of diminishing his fascination for her, the arm's length she was trying to put between them just intrigued him more. It was all kinds of bad because relationships were not his specialty. So far he'd been less than successful in staying uninvolved, and one wrong move could cost him the community approval he needed to make this career move and the life he wanted a success.

Now that he had a diagnosis, it was time to come up with the treatment. So far, he had nothing.

Potter's Ice Cream Parlor was hosting a fundraiser for Blackwater Lake High School's football team, and Jill had just finished her two-hour volunteer shift. She was grateful for the break because her hands ached from nonstop scooping. It was standing-room only except for Maggie Potter. Her early labor pains were under control, but she was under obstetrician's orders to stay off her feet and was sitting at a table for two in the center of the room. Her job was to collect cash donations from folks who were watching their calories but still wanted to help out.

Jill sat in the empty chair across from her friend. "You should be at home with your feet up."

"At least I'm off them." Maggie was a pretty brunette, petite and fragile-looking. Her beautiful brown eyes were sad and hadn't lost their haunted look since she'd gotten the news that her husband had died in Afghanistan. "It's been a week since I saw the doctor, and doing nothing is driving me crazy."

"You have to put crazy on a back burner and take care of that baby."

"I'm doing my best. Now that Dan is gone, there's nothing more important than this baby. I have to make sure a part of his father goes on." She settled her palms on the baby bump. "You can put your own maternal instinct on a back burner because I called the doctor for permission. He said it's okay to be out of the house as long as I'm taking it easy. If I get wild and end up behind the counter, Brady has orders to pick me up bodily and take me home to solitary confinement."

Jill laughed. "So it's your big brother's day to watch you."

"Every day is his day, poor guy." The sadness in her eyes deepened. "He's running the parlor right now, until the baby is born and I'm back on my feet."

"He's a really good guy."

Jill had often wondered why she hadn't fallen for Brady O'Keefe in high school instead of Buddy Henderson. The only good thing that jerk had left her was C.J. Other than that, it was a lot of bad memories and no desire to fall in love again. Ever. The one time she'd even thought about it, the doctor took off and she wasn't in the mood to test the theory about third time's the charm.

"It doesn't hurt that Brady owns a successful business of his own. He can structure his time to give me a hand, but he's really stretched thin." Maggie was looking at the door. "Speaking of good-looking men…"

Jill knew by the expression on her friend's face that she was looking at Blackwater Lake's newest doctor. She hadn't seen him since the incident by the lake a few days ago. Thinking about it afterward, she'd been unable to decide if he was a good, softhearted guy or an interfering jerk who wasn't going to be around and had no emotional investment in whether or not C.J. became a responsible adult.

When her friend started to wave him over, Jill protested, "No."

Maggie's eyebrow rose questioningly. "Oh, really?"

"What 'oh, really'?"

"Don't play dumb with me. I've known you too long. What's up with you and your newest tenant?"

"Who says anything is? Can't I just not want to talk to him?"

"Not unless you have your eyesight checked and your head examined," Maggie said, her gaze tracking him as he moved farther into the crowded room. "He's gorgeous and seems really nice. I know everyone in town hates his guts because of what the last doctor did to you, but I believe in giving people the benefit of the doubt."

"Only because he's got an ice-cream obsession and is a good customer," Jill retorted.

"That doesn't hurt. But, for goodness' sake, he's a bachelor without children and is here to support the football team. That gets a check mark in the 'pro' column." The sadness in her eyes deepened. "Danny loved playing football for Blackwater Lake High. It was his idea to do this annual fundraiser, and I'll defend anyone who is here to support it." Unexpectedly a small smile turned up the corners of her beautiful mouth. "And by the looks of it he's not just buying for himself."

Jill turned and followed her friend's gaze, noting that there were four kids with Adam in line. Reading the body language, she could see that he was relaying questions and answers from volunteers behind the counter and the boys giving their orders. When each sundae was ready, he handed it over to the child.

"Wow," Maggie said.

"What?" Jill turned back to her.

"He's buying the Mag-nificent Mocha and the Dan-dee Delight, the two most expensive things I have."

Jill knew her husband had created and named them after the two of them. She also knew Adam was trying to win over the community and wondered if this was a bribe or he was being extra nice to Maggie. She hated being that cynical. It would be shallow, self-centered and just plain wrong to compare what she'd experienced to Maggie's incomprehensible loss, but something had died inside Jill, and a couple of men were responsible. Now she looked at everything involving men through a magnifying glass made of skepticism.

"I hope the kids don't get sick," Maggie said, watching the boys juggle their treats over to a table while the doctor paid the bill. "Now Adam is looking around for a place to sit."

"Are you going to do a running commentary on his movements all night?"

Maggie folded her arms and rested them on her ballooning belly. "Someone took a crabby pill. Maybe you need something to sweeten your disposition."

"If you're suggesting ice cream, I've already had mine."

"Finishing C.J.'s doesn't count."

Jill automatically looked for her son and saw him in a far corner with Tyler Dixon and his dad. There was a part of her that always breathed a sigh of relief when she could see him happy and healthy.

"I may have finished his, but that means we both took one for the team." The comment made her friend smile, and that was enough to sweeten her disposition.

"Hello, ladies."

"Adam." Maggie's voice was dripping with friendly and topped with welcome. "Why don't you pull up a chair?"

Even if Maggie hadn't announced him, Jill would know that voice anywhere. It was deep and rugged and seemed to have a direct line to her heart, kicking up the beat until surely everyone in the noisy, crowded room could hear.

Jill saw the mischievous gleam in the other woman's eyes. It momentarily blocked out the sad, and for that she was grateful. When he moved into her view she said, "Hi, Adam. Join us."

He glanced from one to the other. "You two looked serious about something. I don't want to interrupt any soul-baring confessions."

Jill was doing her level best to keep this guy from searing her soul and wanted to tell him he was absolutely interrupting them, but had a bad feeling Maggie wanted him to sit down. There was probably no way to avoid it, so she sweetened her disposition and aimed all that sugar in his direction.

"We were just chatting," she said to him. "Nothing important. Sit with us."

"Okay." A faint look of surprise flitted across his face just before he grabbed a recently vacated chair from a nearby table. He pulled it over and sat. "How's the mother-to-be?"

"Doing nothing, as ordered, and teetering on the edge of insanity," Maggie answered.

He laughed. "Apparently the edge agrees with you. Glowing is an understatement."

Definitely he was being extra nice to her, Jill thought. "Is that your official medical opinion, Doctor?"

"It is." Then he studied her. "And you look like a woman who could use a day off."

When he turned his baby blues on her, she felt the effects just short of her soul. Then the meaning of his words sank in. Tired? Bags under her eyes? She looked like something the cat yakked up?

Glancing at her best friend's amused expression, Jill knew Maggie knew what she was thinking. Before she could decide how to sugarcoat her response, Mayor Loretta Goodson stopped beside the table.

"Hi, Jill." Her Honor was a tall, slender, attractive woman who made the mid-forties look like the new thirty. Her shiny, shoulder-length brown hair was stylishly cut in layers and her jeans, white blouse and navy blazer struck just the right balance between friendly elected official and professional businesswoman. As far as anyone knew, she'd never been married and when she looked at the pregnant lady, there was a mirror image of sadness in her gray eyes. "You look good, Maggie."

"I feel good."

The mayor nodded, then extended her hand to Adam. "We haven't met, Doctor. Mayor Loretta Goodson."

"It's a pleasure," he said.

"How are you settling in?"

He hesitated just a second before responding, "Making a change is always a challenge."

Loretta nodded. "Folks in Blackwater Lake pride themselves on loyalty."

"And they're good at it," he said wryly.

Jill knew it was a veiled reference to everyone in town freezing him out to protect her.

"Their attitude will change. Doing physicals at no charge for the football team helps," the mayor said. "And it's important for everyone to accept you. I was elected to grow the tax base here in town, and to do that we need to attract business. People work in businesses and they'll need services, like health care."

Now Jill felt really guilty and personally responsible for hindering town expansion. On her account Adam was being treated as if he'd already screwed up just for being a doctor who rented her apartment.

The mayor smiled at him. "It occurs to me that you might want to do a booth at the Harvest Festival next month."

"I don't make quilts or pickle cucumbers," he joked.

"Health screenings were more what I had in mind."

"Taking blood pressure, cholesterol and diabetes checks. Eye exams," he said, thinking out loud.

"We could set you up between the pumpkin pies and corn dogs," she teased.

"That'll make folks love me," he said ruefully. "A terrible warning."

Loretta laughed. "Just a healthy reminder. It would be great exposure and a good way for people to get to know you."

"Sounds like an idea, Madam Mayor. Who should I talk to about setting it all up?"

"Calvin Johnson." She pointed out a man across the room who had his arm draped across one of the teenage football players. "I'll take you over there right now and make introductions."

"I'd like that. I actually came over here to give you a donation for the team," he said to Maggie. "Give me a couple minutes and I'll be back with a check." Then he looked down at Jill. "See you later."

Speechless, Jill smiled and nodded, then watched him walk away. The information about contributing his medical expertise to the kids was new, unexpected and something the last doctor hadn't done. She understood that the money he'd spent tonight was about buying town approval and it was for a good cause. But free physicals was time-consuming, not to mention above and beyond the call of duty. That made it awfully difficult not to respect the gesture. And like him for it.

It was a disconcerting realization. How could she hold out against the new doctor who went out of his way for the high school football team and was extra nice to a pregnant war widow? What could a girl do to put up a defense against a man like that?

Somewhere between talking to the mayor and sweetening her disposition, Jill had misplaced the hostility that was her best weapon.

Chapter Four

Adam drove home from the clinic along Lakeview Road, and it hadn't been called that for no reason. The street curved around the lake and the view was pretty spectacular. Hence the name. The thing was, no matter how difficult his day, looking at the sparkling expanse of water and the tree-covered mountains of Montana seemed to suck out the bad mood and pump up his spirits. At least that part of his career move had gone according to plan. As for the rest, time would tell.

He stopped at the two side-by-side Quonset hut-shaped boxes on the road leading to the house and retrieved his mail, then pulled into the driveway and parked beside Jill's small, older, gas-efficient car. Somehow it suited her, he thought, copper-colored and compact. But her curves were the kind that kept him up nights because his imagination tried to fill in the blanks of what it would feel like to explore her.

After turning off the SUV, he headed for the house.

Rounding the corner, he spotted C.J. sitting on the front step with a baseball glove beside him. His bony elbows dug into his knees, and his face rested in his hands.

Adam stopped in front of him. "Hey, champ."

"Hi, Dr. Adam."

"What's going on?"

"Nothin'."

"You didn't get sick from all that ice cream you ate last night, did you?"

The boy shook his head.

"Are you okay?"

He nodded.

This wasn't the never-still, never-silent child Adam had come to know. Something was up with him. "Why are you sitting here by yourself?"

"My mom is doing homework. She told me to go outside and play."

Homework? A question for another time. "So, how come you're not playing?"

C.J. shrugged. "There's nobody to play with."

And there was the downside of living on Lakeview Road near Blackwater Lake. The land wasn't developed and there weren't any kids right next door to hang out with like a tract home neighborhood. The closest house was almost a mile down the road. Even if a kid C.J.'s age lived there, a vigilant mom like Jill wouldn't be comfortable letting him walk there on his own. Besides being cautious, she was a busy working mom, not a chauffeur, and badly needed a day off.

C.J. looked at him. "Will you play catch with me?"

Adam recognized the pleading in those sad brown eyes so like his mother's. Memories of all the times his father had come home and he'd asked the very same question came back to him now. But his father, the Nobel Prize–winning econo-mist, was always too busy or tired to play.

"Sure, champ. I'd love to throw the ball around."

C.J. sat up straighter. "Really?"

He nodded. "Playing catch is one of my favorite things to do."

The boy jumped up, then froze. "Do you have a mitt?"

"No." Adam held back a grin. "But if you go easy throwing the ball, I think I can handle it."

"Okay."

They stood several feet apart on the grass to the side of the walkway. The sun was just going behind the mountain; it wouldn't be light for long.

Adam braced his feet shoulder-length apart, bent his knees and held out his hands. "Ready."

The kid threw the ball wide. "Sorry, Dr. Adam. I don't throw so good."

"No problem. Just takes practice." Moving to the side, he bent to pick up the ball and realized it was hard rubber, not a hardball. He gave it a soft underhanded toss back that was right on the money but fell between C.J.'s hands.

"I'm really bad at catchin', too."

"You'll get the hang of it. Just keep your eye on the ball, champ."

"Okay." There was still a discouraged, defeated tone in his voice.

"How was school today?" Adam lunged a foot to his right and managed a bare-handed catch of the ball.

"Not good."

He tossed it back through the kid's hands again. "What happened?"

"I didn't get picked for the baseball team." There was a world of hurt in his voice. "The yard duty lady told 'em they had to let me play, but I didn't want to then."

Adam was angry even though he knew this kind of crap was all part of growing up. This was the part that built character, but it didn't come without pain. What ticked him off most was that there wasn't any injectable medication or pill, or words, to make that pain better. Then C.J. threw the ball over his head and he jogged over to pick it up.

"That sucks." He met the boy's gaze and said, "Did you say anything to your mom about it?"

"No. When I do it makes her sad."

"It's pretty cool that you're taking care of her." The little hero already had enough character to be the man in his mother's life and protect her. She'd done a great job with him on her own. "Was your friend Tyler there when they were picking teams?"

"Nope. He was playin' soccer."

"So you like baseball better?"

"Yeah, but I'm not very good at it."

Adam held his hands out in front of him to give the kid a target for his throw. This time the ball came right to him. "Says who?"

He shrugged. "I didn't get picked 'cuz they said I can't catch or throw or hit very good."

"Keep your eye on the ball," Adam said, then gently lobbed it practically into the mitt.

C.J. closed the glove and put his hand over it to hold on to the ball. He jumped up and down. "I did it!"

"Nice job. Way to go, champ. See? It just takes some practice."

"This is fun!"

It was, Adam realized. Watching a child blossom with a little attention was the most fun he'd had in a long time. For the next ten minutes they tossed the ball back and forth with more drops than catches, but success couldn't necessarily be measured by runs scored. The kid had his enthusiasm back and some self-esteem, too. If that wasn't a victory, he didn't know what was.

Finally Adam realized they'd lost the light and it was time to call it a day. "I think it's getting too dark, C.J. Better go inside."

"I can turn on the porch light," C.J. offered eagerly.

"It won't be enough."

"O-okay." He dragged his feet and moved closer, then looked up. "Dr. Adam?"

"Yeah?"

"Do you need help unpackin' any more boxes? You got any stuff to put away?"

Adam grinned at the transparent attempt to prolong the hanging out. "Actually, I think I'm all settled. But if I find something I missed and need help with it, I'll let you know."

"Got anything to do now?"

"Not really. I just have to go find something for dinner," he said.

"We're havin' my favorite," C.J. said.

"What's that?"

"Hot dogs with mashed potatoes on 'em."

"Sounds good." To his credit Adam didn't shudder, although it was probably too dark to see even if he did.

"If you don't have any food, you can come to my house and eat."

Adam figured that would go over like mouse droppings in the pantry. Jill had made it pretty clear that he should avoid C.J. and her. "I don't think your mom would be happy about that."

"She won't mind."

Adam glanced at the front window and the light inside. The view on his drive home, spectacular though it was, couldn't fill the simmering sense of loneliness his landlady's window generated in him as he passed by it every night. He knew she and her son were inside laughing, talking and being together. She'd smiled at him last night at the ice-cream parlor and seemed friendlier, but it could have been for the benefit of the mayor and her friend Maggie. It wasn't necessarily a reaction he could afford to trust or test too far.

"I don't know, champ. It's probably not a good idea for me to come over without asking her. There might not be enough food. Maybe another time."

"Nah. She always tells me I can have friends over anytime I want to. And we always have enough hot dogs."

The light from the window outlined the eagerness in C.J.'s expression. This child had been rejected once today, and there was no way to prevent that, but a yes from him now would avoid two rejections in a row. Adam didn't have the heart to disappoint him.

If she had a problem with him showing up, it would be her responsibility to explain to her son why. Would that put her on the spot? Heck yes. But maybe it was time to shake things up. Jill needed to get used to the fact that he wasn't going anywhere.

C.J. tugged on his hand. "Please say yes, Dr. Adam."

"Okay. You talked me into it. What time?"

"We eat at six."

"I'll be there."

And that would give him just enough time to run an errand first.

Jill pulled the hot dogs topped with mashed potatoes out of the oven and set the cookie sheet holding them on top of the stove. Her mother had come up with this simple dinner after Jill's father had left. Money was tight and it was especially sinful to throw food away.

Dottie had called the meals clean-out-the-refrigerator-for-two and sometimes they involved creative ways to use vegetables, potatoes and whatever leftover meat hadn't entered an altered state that resembled a science experiment gone terribly wrong. Dinners weren't always a culinary triumph, but hot dogs with mashed potatoes was one of Jill's favorites and fortunately her son liked it, too.

There was a knock on the front door followed quickly by the galumphing sound of C.J.'s sneakers coming down the hallway from his bedroom. "I'll get it," he hollered.

"No!" She rushed out of the kitchen to beat him to the front door. It was unusual to get visitors out here by the lake, especially this time of the evening. "We don't know who's out there. I'm not expecting anyone."

"I am."

In front of the door she stared down at her little guy, an uneasy feeling knotting her insides. "Just who are you expecting?"

"Dr. Adam."

Before she could quiz him further, there was another, more forceful knock. Jill peeked through the shutter and, sure enough, Adam was standing there on the porch.

"Open the door, Mom. Don't make him stand out there all night." C.J.'s tone sounded suspiciously like hers. "You're being kind of rude."

And so the child becomes the parent. Unfortunately he was right, and not just about this moment. At the very least, she'd been borderline rude since Adam expressed interest in renting her upstairs apartment. That's not how she was raised.

"You're right, C.J." She opened the door and started to say hello, but the flowers and bottle of wine Adam was holding kept her speechless. The front porch was dark and unwelcoming, kind of like her, and when she peeked out, she hadn't seen what he was holding.

"Hi." Adam smiled down at C.J. "Hey, buddy."

Jill finally found her voice. "This is a surprise."

"I came for dinner."

"I 'vited him," her son added.

She looked down at him. "You should have asked me first. So I could be prepared. I'd have made more food." And better food.

"If this isn't a good time, I'll take a rain check." Adam held out the flowers, daisies mixed with baby's breath, and the bottle of wine. Numbly she took them from him.

"It's okay, Mom. Dr. Adam can have my hot dog. I'll make myself a peanut butter and jelly." Her son must have seen the protest forming because he added, "You always tell me we hafta help people who don't have anything, and Dr. Adam doesn't have any dinner. He told me he had to go find something."

Jill had often said that herself, but C.J. was taking the statement literally. This wasn't the time to explain, especially because she was actually pretty proud of him. All her preaching and lecturing had produced fruit, although it was probably the most inopportune time for the most inconvenient man.

"You're welcome to stay." She met Adam's amused gaze. "It's not fancy. An old family recipe."

"C.J. told me what's on the menu."

She closed the door with her hip because her hands were full. "And you're here in spite of full disclosure."

"I keep telling you I don't cut-and-run. Or scare easily."

That made one of them because the smile he dropped on her was equal parts charm and sex appeal, which scared her a lot. It was unnerving how easily, how fast, the combination stole her breath away, but she was stuck now.

"I'll set another place at the table and put a couple more hot dogs in the oven."

"Come and see my room, Dr. Adam." C.J. tugged on his hand.

"Lead the way, champ."

Jill half expected him to brush off her son the way the

last doctor had done. It still made her spitting mad that the jerk had broken C.J.'s heart even though he'd never gone out of his way to spend time with her son. The fallout could be worse if her boy formed a relationship with Adam. But she was borrowing trouble and it was becoming a habit.

In the kitchen, Jill put the already-cooked hot dogs in foil and set them on a warming tray. She made more of her specialty, then set out another plate and eating utensils on the round oak table. The flowers went into the crystal vase that had been her mother's and she set them in the center of the place settings. Part of her was hoping to hide behind the arrangement.

Looking at the label on the wine, she wondered if cabernet sauvignon paired well with hot dogs. Smiling, she opened the bottle and poured the deep red liquid into the two glasses she'd bought for a dollar apiece at the thrift store on Main Street.

After fixing a salad, she was just about to call out that dinner was ready when C.J. tugged the affable doctor into the room and announced, "Me and Dr. Adam are hungry, Mom."

"Then it's a good thing dinner is ready." She looked at Adam. "Don't say I didn't warn you."

"You're gonna like it, Dr. Adam. This is my favorite food."

"I thought ice cream was number one." Jill watched her son plop his tush on a chair where the place setting had a glass of wine.

"Ice cream is my favorite dessert. And I'm sittin' here tonight."

"Okay." Jill switched the wine with his tumbler of milk. "But that doesn't mean you get a pass on drinking this."

"But, Mom—"

"No buts, Christopher John. It has calcium and that's good for your bones and teeth."

"Then how come my teeth still fall out?" he grumbled.

"Not all of them." Jill glanced at Adam, who was biting his lip to keep from laughing. That made it harder for her to keep her serious mom-face in place. "Your baby teeth came out to make room for the permanent ones. All the more reason to take care of them because that's all you're going to get. So, drink up or no dessert."

"Yes, ma'am." He took a token sip that left a white mustache.

Jill watched Adam's face as he cut off a bite of hot dog and potato. She'd added slices of cheese to spruce things up a little, but it was still a hot dog.

After swallowing he said, "Not bad."

"Told you," C.J. said, stuffing a too-big piece in his own mouth.

"Chew that carefully," Jill warned. "You're going to choke." When he mumbled something unintelligible she added, "Don't talk with your mouth full."

She took a sip of wine and nodded at their guest who had brought it. "This is really good."

"I'm glad you like it." He pushed the vase of flowers aside to the empty place at the table. "I was surprised to find it at the store in town. It's a label my parents like."

"They have good taste."

"Of course. They're practically perfect. It's not easy being the flawed offspring of such gifted and talented people."

"They must be pretty busy with their demanding careers."

"Mom is starting to cut back some."

"What about your dad?"

"When he isn't winning Nobel Prizes for economics, he teaches college classes on the subject."

"Wow." Feeling like a particularly dim country bumpkin, she took another sip of wine. "How do they feel about you moving to Blackwater Lake?"

He'd already polished off one of his hot dogs and a good portion of salad. "How can I put this delicately?"

"Careful." She glanced at her son, who was soaking up every word. "There's a minor present."

"Understood. I'll say it this way. My mother isn't subtle. She never misses an opportunity to ask if I'm bored yet with my Daniel Boone imitation and ready to move back to Dallas."

"You're leaving?" C.J.'s voice rose an octave, a big clue that he wouldn't be happy about that.

"No, champ. I'm staying put. I like it here."

He was looking at Jill when he said it, and there was mischief in his eyes. A wicked expression that made her want to get into trouble with him. Even if he invited her, she didn't have to say yes. For tonight she could just enjoy conversation with an adult male and not be in danger of making a mistake. No matter how often he swore that sticking around was the plan, she knew better than to picture him in her tomorrow, let alone forever. One night didn't have to cost her.

"C.J. tells me you were doing homework." There was a question in Adam's voice.

"When did he say that?"

C.J. put his milk glass back on the table. "Dr. Adam played catch with me."

"I hope he didn't bother you," she said quickly.

"It was fun." Adam smiled at the boy. "He's got a lot of potential."

"Yes, he does."

The wickedness faded from Adam's eyes and she had a feeling that her son had confided in him earlier. Now wasn't the time to ask what was said.

"I was doing an assignment. I'm taking online classes for a bachelor's degree in business. Better late than never." She shrugged. "I was in junior college intending to transfer, but then C.J. was born. My mom got sick. And I had to put school on hold for a while."

Adam put his knife and fork on the empty plate. "I can't think of a better way to show your son how much value you put on education and a work ethic."

"I never thought about it like that." His words started a glow inside her. "Honestly, I just got thrown into the deep end of the pool and continued to run the marina like my mother did. The classes are to make sure I'm doing it right."

"Doing what right, Mom?" C.J. couldn't hold back a big yawn.

"Making sure you get enough sleep, big guy. Time for your shower."

"But Dr. Adam's here. And I didn't have my dessert yet. I ate all my dinner, too. See?" He held up the empty plate for inspection. "And I'm havin' so much fun. It's almost as good as goin' out to dinner." He looked at Adam. "We never get to except for special stuff 'cuz it's awful expensive."

Jill figured that after six years she should be used to her son sharing embarrassing aspects of their life, but she wasn't. She didn't want to be pitied, especially by Adam Stone.

She ignored the statement. "You can have some ice cream after you get ready for bed, C.J."

"I'll be here when you're finished," Adam promised.

C.J. looked at her, gauging his response. "Is this one of those times that no means no 'cuz you're the mom?"

"Yes."

"Okay. But—" He pointed at Adam. "Don't go. I'll hurry."

"Be sure to wash your feet," she called after him.

When they were alone, she looked at Adam and saw that his shoulders were shaking. She burst out laughing, too.

"He's something else." Adam chuckled. "Really a bright kid."

"Tell me about it. Makes mothering a challenge." She stood and started stacking plates.

"I'll give you a hand." He carried his own plate to the sink.

Jill followed and stood beside him, looking up. "Did he tell you about not getting picked for a team at recess?"

"He said you didn't know about that."

"His teacher called to clue me in, just in case he was upset."

"He was," Adam confirmed.

"And so am I. I'd like to throttle the little stinkers, but it's not in anyone's best interest."

"I have to agree with you there."

"Part of being a mother is stepping aside to let your child fight his own battles. Or fall on his face. To handle it in his own way." She met his gaze. "I'm a little concerned that he's more upset than he let on because of talking to you about what happened."

"It was a guy thing." Adam rested a hip against the counter and studied her. "That was him trying to protect you. He said it makes you sad."

"Of course it does. No one wants to see their child left out—" Emotion choked off her words, and tears burned her eyes.

"Jill—"

He touched her shoulder and something that felt a lot like an electric current arced between them. The sadness vanished, replaced by a hot, spicy sizzle. She didn't know which one of them moved first, but all of a sudden his arms were around her and their lips were a whisper apart.

Chapter Five

Before Jill could even whisper "no," Adam's mouth was on hers. His lips were soft and he smelled so good—manly and spicy and sexy. In a heartbeat the contact grew more intense and he wrapped his arms around her waist and pressed her body to his, her breasts flat against his hard chest. Her breathing was shallow, fast and mingled with his as the harsh sound of it filled her small kitchen.

Her pulse was throbbing and the blood pounded in her ears as he kissed the living daylights out of her. Liquid heat poured through her and settled in places that proved her feminine parts still worked.

When he traced her top lip with his tongue, she opened eagerly, letting him explore and take what he wanted. Happily, willingly she went along for the ride. She slid her palms up and over his chest, soaking up that exquisitely muscular masculine contour. He kissed her over and over, then let his mouth wander to the corner of hers before sliding to her cheek and that take-me-now spot just by her ear. If there was a God, this moment would go on forever.

Adam Stone was rocking her world.

Until he wasn't.

She didn't know which of them had moved first and started it, but there was no doubt who was responsible for ending it. He went still, as if some sound, some thought, breached the sensual haze, bringing the equivalent of a glass of cold water to the face with it.

He took her hands, squeezed tight, then lowered them from his chest. "I'm sorry."

A nanosecond ago she wasn't sorry, but that was beginning to change. From the moment they'd met, her defenses had been in place, with a firm negative repeating over and over in her head. Who knew hot dogs, mashed potatoes and wine were such a powerful aphrodisiac that one touch of his mouth made her his for the taking? It was kind of humiliating.

Jill shook her head, as much to clear it as a disapproving reaction to his words. "You have nothing to be sorry for."

"I shouldn't have done that. It's all my fault." He stood with his back to her sink and dragged his fingers through his hair.

Part of her wanted him to define *it,* but she didn't ask, probably because she didn't want to hear the answer. Taking two steps away from him, she said, "Wow. Words every girl is just dying to hear…being someone's fault."

All hint of charm disappeared from his face, leaving behind an intense expression that looked a lot like self-recrimination. "This isn't a good idea. You. Me." He moved his hand, indicating both of them. "I'm not good at relationships."

"Neither am I." She knew what was coming and couldn't believe he was gallant enough to say what she was thinking.

"I want to be the best family practice doctor possible," he

explained. "To do that I can't be an outsider. This community needs to accept me as one of its own. So far that's not going as well as it could."

"On account of me," she said.

"Not your fault I'm paying the price for another guy's mistake. I can get past that as long as I don't screw up, too."

"Right." Jill forced a sunny smile that threatened to crack her face. *Please let this conversation be over.* "I see what you mean."

He didn't look convinced. "I think we can be good friends, but anything else has the potential to go badly based on my history. That could get awkward, complicated and counterproductive to what I'm trying to accomplish."

"You're absolutely right." Her tone had more enthusiasm than sincerity. "You may be bad at relationships, but I'll go you one better. I've already lived this one. I can give you a blow-by-blow of how this will play out. Spoiler alert—it's not pretty."

For some reason her agreement intensified his frown. "So we're on the same page. Best to sidestep this land mine."

"Absolutely." She caught her bottom lip between her teeth. "But I have a favor to ask."

"Anything."

"Mayor Goodson says good health care is important for area growth. I can do friends with you." She blew out a long breath. "But don't pretend it just to fit in."

"I'd never do that." Frustration and anger wrapped around the words.

"That's what the last doctor said." She held up her hand to stop him when he started to protest. "There's one more thing."

"That's two favors."

"It's important."

He nodded. "Okay. What?"

"Don't start anything with C.J. Don't pretend to be his friend. Don't play catch and pay attention to him if you're going to drop him like a hot rock. He's vulnerable. And you may have noticed that he's hungry for male companionship—"

"I'd never hurt him. I'm not leaving." A muscle worked in his jaw as his fingers curled into his palms. "*You* may have noticed that I'm doing everything possible to build a life here."

She stared at him for several moments and realized he wasn't faking the same frustration she was feeling at calling off that kiss. That made her feel much better and slightly more willing to believe him.

Then she heard the sound of bare feet running through the living room before C.J. hollered, "Mommy, I'm all clean."

Call her naive, but she didn't believe Adam had planned to put moves on her tonight. If so, he'd have waited until C.J. was in bed. There was some comfort in that, but not nearly enough.

With wet hair and wearing superhero pajamas, the little boy appeared in the doorway and came to a sudden halt. "Dr. Adam, you're still here."

The doctor's eyes never left hers when he said, "I told you I'd stay."

"Cool." C.J. stared first at her, then Adam. "How come you guys look weird?"

"Maybe you still have water in your eyes?" she said, trying to deflect with humor.

"Nope. I dried real good. And I washed my feet. See?" He held up a foot and would have toppled sideways if she hadn't caught him.

"Nice job, kiddo."

Better than her. She was a complete failure at the objectives for which she'd been preparing. She wasn't supposed to crumple like a used tissue the first time Dr. Adam Stone showed the slightest interest. Ironically they were in complete agreement about how unwise it was to pursue anything personal, but the disappointment flooding through her took her completely by surprise. Still, what she resented the most was that he'd been the strong one and actually had the willpower to pull away before things got out of control.

"Mom? I want dessert now."

Yeah, Jill thought darkly, there was a lot of that going around.

Adam had thought a strenuous hike in the mountains around Blackwater Lake would relieve the tension coiled like a rattler in his gut. Three hours later he walked out of the woods sweaty, tired and more tense than when he'd left. Jill's car was gone, which was both a blessing and curse. He couldn't look forward to seeing her, because she wasn't there, but then the wondering where she'd gone and what she was doing kicked in.

This was nothing new since he'd moved in upstairs. It had just become more intense since he'd kissed her the other night. He needed a tension-relieving activity, and he needed it bad. Specifically something to take his mind off Jill. More specifically her mouth. And to put a finer point on it, the necessity of finding something to keep him from thinking about kissing those full, tempting lips was getting more urgent every day.

If he hadn't slipped up and gone there, it wouldn't be an acute problem now because he wouldn't have any idea about the sweet secrets her mouth had promised. But he did screw up, and doing it again would be an even bigger mistake. So he had to find something to fill his free time.

Adam walked around the front of the house, toward the stairway leading to his apartment. Glancing down at the dock on the lake, he noticed a sign in front of the marina store. Sale—All Fishing Gear Twenty-Five Percent Off. He hadn't cast a line in the water since his time at camp. Maybe it was time he did.

Fishing could distract him. Die-hard fishermen swore the sport was relaxing and put all your troubles on hold. If nothing else, the smell of lake trout wasn't the least bit like the sweet scent of Jill's soft skin.

It was a plan and he went to the little store to take action. There was a display of fishing poles on the wooden walkway beside the door, but they all looked the same as far as he was concerned. Different-sized sutures or medical equipment, he was your guy, but this was Greek to him.

He walked inside and looked around. Not much had changed since the day he'd hung out with C.J. by the lake. The biggest difference was that signs were everywhere advertising markdowns. His guess was the summer merchandise had to be sold before winter set in. Anything not moved out would have to be stored.

Adam didn't see anyone minding the shop and noticed there was another door on the opposite side that looked out onto the marina. He stepped outside and saw Brewster Smith hosing down fishing poles, rubber boots, tackle boxes and an ice chest beneath a sign that said Equipment Rental. "Hi." Adam raised his hand in greeting.

The other man nodded, but didn't say anything, then turned his attention back to what he was doing.

"Journey of a thousand miles…" Adam muttered, then walked over. The sun was shining in a clear blue sky and pine trees covering the mountains looked even greener. "Beautiful day."

Brewster looked up. "Yeah. Winter will be here before too long."

Mr. Glass-Half-Empty, Adam thought. "How's business?"

"Same as always this time of year."

The older man was wearing a blue work shirt with the sleeves rolled to the elbows and faded-to-almost-white jeans. His scuffed boots were well-worn and wet, along with the one knee resting on the ground. His thick gray hair could use a trim, as could the beard, and the skin showing was leathery, the sign of a man who'd labored outside for most of his life.

Adam wanted to recommend a sunblock with SPF fifty for face, neck, hands and even the skin under the shirt. He didn't say anything, figuring they needed to bond a little more first.

"Looks like there's a big sale going on," he said, setting the bonding process in motion.

"Noticed that, did you?" There was irony in the pale blue gaze the older man turned on him. "It's a comfort to know you can read."

Adam took the high road and ignored the sarcasm. "Might be a good time to buy a fishing pole."

"Rod." Brewster used a bristle brush on one of the rubber boots.

"Excuse me?"

"Fishing *rod*," he said. "Only greenhorns or city slickers call it a pole."

"Good to know." Adam silently counted to ten, determined to maintain a cheerful and unruffled appearance. "I'm thinking of taking up fishing. I hear it's relaxing."

"Where'd you hear that?"

What the hell difference did it make? "I'm not sure. Around."

"Hmm," was the only response.

"Maybe you could recommend equipment for a beginner?"

"Best advice?" Brewster looked up and there wasn't a hint of friendliness in his expression. "Just rent or go cheap."

"Because it's less complex and easier to use?"

"Nope. Just practical."

"Why?"

"Best not to put a lot of money into something you'll leave behind after pulling up stakes." Brewster went to work cleaning the other rubber boot.

Adam refused to rise to the bait, no pun intended, but an appropriate metaphor in a fishing store. "I'm here for the long haul and money's not an issue. What do you think I should start with?"

"Depends."

I'll bite, Adam thought. Again with the fishing figure of speech. "On what?"

"On what your intentions are."

This guy was already looking to cut his heart out with a spoon. No way would Adam try to bond over the fact that he'd kissed Jill and was now looking for a way to forget about her. Brewster would never understand that Adam's intentions were to fix the mistake, that it was best for both of them. And C.J.

He remembered Jill saying that she could give him a blow-by-blow of what would happen if they tried a relationship. But, damn it, he wasn't the last doctor and it bugged him that he was painted with the jerk brush. There was no point in challenging her because he wasn't willing to start something just to prove her wrong. He wasn't going to take the risk.

"Define *intentions,*" he finally said.

"You planning to hang around and look busy or actually catch something?" Brewster rested his forearm on his thigh. "If you're figuring on volume, there's trolling gear."

Adam had a fairly high I.Q. He'd made it through medical school at the top of his class, after all. But Jill Beck's self-appointed protector was making this clear as mud. On purpose. "I'm not following."

"There's simple cane rods—some call 'em bank rods."

"Why?"

Again irony in the older man's expression. "Because you stand on the bank of the water to use it."

"Ah." Adam had actually guessed that. "What else?"

"Some rods and trolling equipment are meant to be used on a boat, either anchored or moving."

"I see." Adam nodded. "I hadn't thought about a boat. Is the fishing better in deep lake water?"

"Maybe. Maybe not."

"How does one go about buying a boat?"

Brewster rubbed a leathery hand across his neck. "Got some docked here at the marina that folks are trying to sell. But they're mostly bigger, for longer trips."

The implication was that anything for sale here would be too much for Adam to handle, and that was probably true. "Is there something smaller that you know about?"

The older man reached over and turned off the hose at the spigot. "Rowboat."

"Can I see it?"

"Over there." He cocked his thumb, indicating the big, open area of the dock behind the store.

Adam walked over and saw a tarp tented over something. Since there was nothing else around, he lifted the canvas to have a look. Underneath was a stack of wood and the skeleton of what appeared to be a rowboat-under-construction. Obviously the older man was messing with him. Another frustrating moment in an increasingly frustrating conversation.

Moving back to where the man was coiling the hose, Adam struggled with his patience. "Looks like it will be a boat when it grows up."

"Been like that for a while," Brewster confirmed. "Started it on commission for that doctor who skipped town. He left Jill blowing in the wind for the money she put out on materials. At least she kept the deposit."

"Good for her." Adam nodded thoughtfully. "Might be

nice to have something like that in the spring. Can you finish it for me? I'll pay up front."

"You're still here in the spring we can talk about it. No point in wasting energy, or storing something that won't get used."

Adam's turn-the-other-cheek attitude was just about played out. He had one nerve left, and Brewster Smith was standing on it. "I'll be here in the spring."

"Heard that before."

"That's it." Adam's temper snapped. The cheerful well dried up and he was too pissed off to care about bonding or diplomacy. He took a step closer to the other man. "I'm sick and tired of everyone in Blackwater Lake assuming I'm just like the guy who hurt Jill."

Brewster didn't back down. His steely-eyed gaze never wavered as he planted his hands on his hips. "And I'm sick of seeing that girl cry over men who aren't worth spit. It's not happening again. Not on my watch."

Adam decided not to waste his breath repeating the fact that he wasn't going anywhere. He said something else that was just as true. "I'm not going to make her cry."

"I'll believe that when I see it. And make no mistake. I'm watching you," he added before walking away.

Adam knew the older man would also be passing along anything he saw to Jill. He blew out a long breath as he stood outside in the sun. It was hard enough to prove yourself in a new job, but he had the added pressure of proving to the whole town that he wasn't the other guy. The entire population of Blackwater Lake was watching him, waiting for him to screw up.

If he gave in to temptation and kissed Jill again, there was little doubt in his mind that he'd take her to bed. That would be a slippery slope into the relationship pool. After that it was a hop, skip and jump into her wanting more—commitment and vows. That wasn't something he could do again.

The disappointment had the potential to make her cry, and he'd just sworn not to do that. But if he didn't stop thinking about her, all his promises could go up in smoke, right along with his dream of a life in Blackwater Lake.

If he took her to bed, there was very little doubt that everyone in town would know.

And he would pay.

Chapter Six

Jill walked into Mercy Medical Clinic with C.J. even though it was the last place she wanted to be, for so many reasons. C.J. was holding a towel to his injured chin, which had bled on his shirt and sneakers. His freckled face was dirty from playing outside after school, and tears had made tracks through the grime.

They walked over to the flat desk in what was once the living room of the converted Victorian house. The receptionist, Liz Carpenter, was a pretty brunette in her twenties.

She smiled sympathetically. "Got a boo-boo, big guy?"

C.J. nodded solemnly and his mouth quivered. "Mommy says it might need stitches."

Jill looked down and saw tears pooling in his eyes again. Her heart squeezed painfully as it always did when her child was hurting and scared. She wasn't sure which hurts were the worst—physical or emotional—but hated both with a fierce passion fueled by maternal instinct.

"Thanks for getting us in, Liz. I know it's past time for you to go home." Clinic hours were from eight to five and Jill's watch had said six-thirty when she'd pulled the car into a parking space outside.

The receptionist waved her hand in a don't-worry-about-it gesture. "We ran way behind schedule today. You're not the first emergency. I'm used to it. Happens all the time."

"Well, I appreciate it. And hopefully it's not a problem."

"Nope. I checked with Dr. Stone and mentioned C.J. is the patient. He seemed really concerned. Does C.J. need to lie down?"

"No." The panicky tone said he'd rather put off going into an exam room for as long as possible.

"Okay, then." She indicated the chairs in the waiting area. "Just have a seat. The doctor is with his last patient now. It won't be long."

Jill smiled automatically even though crying was what she badly wanted to do, but she had to stay strong for C.J. If she fell apart, this whole thing would be even scarier for him. Putting a hand on his small shoulder, she guided him to an empty row of chairs with a view of the hallway. "Hang in there, kiddo. Before you know it we'll be home and I'll make your favorite dinner."

"Hot dogs and mashed potatoes?"

"Of course." Would she ever make that again without thinking about Adam and what had happened after dinner? That kiss was epic, at least in her experience. Not epic enough, though, if he could back off so easily.

For so many reasons Jill hoped she was wrong about the gash on her son's chin needing stitches. First and foremost she didn't want him to go through any more trauma. And she'd give almost anything to avoid seeing Adam, anything except take C.J. to the hospital that was so far away, which was her only other choice.

Then there was the fact that she hadn't seen Adam since the night he'd kissed her *and* taken it back, which was a personal worst for her. Other men had kissed her, but not one had asked to be friends after doing it.

She wasn't sure if friendship could be pulled off, but it was best to try. Maintaining the appropriate level of hostility to neutralize his charm was an energy suck and she didn't have much to spare.

"Do you want to look at a magazine?" she asked, glancing at the stack on the end table beside her.

C.J. sat stiffly, still holding the cloth to his chin. "No."

She knew his arm had to be getting tired and this was probably as good a time as any to get a good look at the injury. It had been hardly more than a glance at the house. Her first instinct was to stop the bleeding and she'd grabbed the kitchen towel from a drawer. C.J. was crying, scared and wouldn't lower the cloth to let her examine his chin.

"Can I look at your boo-boo?"

"No! Don't touch it." His voice was just this side of a meltdown, which didn't bode well for letting the doctor have a peek, which was the whole reason they were here.

"Okay."

Just then she heard a door open down the hall. There were footsteps on the wooden floor and a murmured conversation that grew louder. Adam appeared in the doorway with Brewster Smith's wife.

Jill shouldn't be surprised, but she was. "Hildie."

"Hey, what are you two doing here?" The older, gray-haired woman smiled and sat in a chair next to C.J. A quick look and she figured out the reason for the visit. "What happened, honey?"

"I fell and hit my chin. Don't touch it," he warned.

"Don't even want to see it," Hildie said with a shudder. She looked at Jill. "Are you holding up okay?"

What other choice did she have? "Yes."

"That's my girl." Hildie reached over and patted her hand. "Do you need me to stay?"

"No. It's getting late."

"Tell me about it. Brew's dinner is not going to be on time tonight." She glanced at Adam as if he were personally responsible.

He smiled, but it looked tired around the edges. "Don't forget to have that prescription filled, Mrs. Smith."

"Are you sick?" Jill asked the older woman.

"No." There was a defensiveness in her voice. "Just out of sorts. I swear there's a pill these days for everything from putting you to sleep to helping a man perform."

Adam laughed. "Some of them actually improve your quality of life. I promise the one I prescribed will do that for you."

"Uh-huh." Clearly Hildie wasn't convinced.

"And I'd like to see you for a follow-up." Obviously he wasn't easily intimidated.

"I'll make an appointment if you're still here," she said skeptically.

Jill didn't miss the way Adam's mouth pulled tight, and it was the first time she'd seen any sign that even subtle comparisons with the last doctor irritated him.

Still his voice was nothing but pleasant when he said, "Then go ahead and make the appointment now. Save yourself a phone call."

Hildie sniffed, and then her face softened when she looked at C.J. "Be a brave boy. Next time you stay with Brew and me I'll bake your favorite cookies."

"The white ones?" As opposed to chocolate chip, which were brown, or the oatmeal raisin variety that he called bumpy.

"Of course."

"Can I help?"

"You always do," Hildie said.

"But this time I want to roll out the dough. And put on a whole bunch of sprinkles."

"It's a deal." The older woman leaned down and gently kissed his forehead, then said to Jill, "Call me when you get home. Let me know how everything goes."

"I will."

Adam cleared his throat. "Follow me, champ."

"Can't you just look at it right here?" C.J. glanced apprehensively at the doorway that led to the exam rooms. "Maybe I don't need stitches. Then Mommy can just put on the anny bactria cream and a superhero Band-Aid."

"He doesn't like going into the room," Adam said, meeting her gaze.

Jill nodded. "The clinic is not his favorite place."

"I can understand that." Adam squatted down and talked directly to C.J. "I could take a look at it here, but the other room has a big light and everything else I need to take good care of you."

"Do I hafta go?" he asked Jill.

"'Fraid so, buddy." She met Adam's gaze and her heart tripped up for reasons that had nothing to do with her son and everything to do with memories of their mouths devouring each other. What kind of mother was she, thinking stuff like that at a time like this?

"How about if I give you a lift?" Adam offered, holding out his arms.

C.J. hesitated for several moments, then said, "I guess."

The doctor picked him up as if he weighed nothing, but Jill knew that wasn't the case. It made her sad that this child she'd easily carried around as an infant was getting too heavy for her to lift at all.

Jill followed them down the hall, the tall, broad-shouldered man in the white lab coat carrying the small boy who had one arm around the strong neck. They went into the first room on the right, where Adam set him down on the paper-covered table. She stood beside her son while Adam washed his hands and then pulled disposable gloves from the box on the counter by the sink.

"Okay, champ, let's have a look."

Those were the magic words that set off her child's classic, clichéd redheaded stubbornness. This time it was fueled by fear. "No. No. Don't touch it."

"I won't." Adam folded his arms over his chest. "Not until you're ready."

"It's gonna hurt. I wanna go home," he wailed.

Jill squeezed his shoulder. "Soon, C.J. Just hold still."

"I can't. I don't wanna hold still."

A look slid into Adam's face as he studied the tantrum-throwing, terror-stricken child. "C.J., have you ever had stitches before?"

Jill was about to answer, but something about the way the doctor was talking directly to her son stopped her. She'd step in if necessary, but maybe the little boy needed to feel as if he was in control.

"C.J.?" Adam prompted.

He nodded. "My knee. I fell on a sprinkler. The other doctor said it wouldn't hurt. But it did. Then Mommy had to change the bandage and she poured watery stuff on it. I looked and it was gross. I told her I was gonna throw up."

"He did warn me," she confirmed. "And he was telling the truth."

"Apparently your son is more honest than the other doctor." His mouth pulled tight and his eyes flashed with anger, but none of that was obvious in his calm voice. "Okay, C.J. Here's the deal."

"I don't want any needles."

"I can't promise anything until you let me look."

"Just look?" the little guy asked skeptically.

"Yes, then we'll talk."

Without a word he slowly lowered the towel from his chin. Jill was standing to the side and could only see the dried blood. Adam moved close enough to inspect the injury.

"What happened?" he asked, looking it over carefully, his arms still folded over his chest. The posture was completely nonthreatening.

"I was runnin' on the front porch and fell. I hit my chin."

"On that old rocking chair?" Adam asked.

"Yeah. The one Mommy got at the garage sale to fix up."

"That rocker isn't all that needs fixing. Your mom is right," Adam said seriously. "You need a couple stitches to close this up."

"No." C.J.'s injured chin took on a stubborn tilt.

"I could put a bandage on it," Adam said slowly. "But it's deep and that means healing will take a long time. And that means no baseball for a while."

"Okay." His tone said he could live with that.

"And there will be a pretty bad scar." Adam stepped back, deliberately giving the child space. "Don't get me wrong. Scars aren't a bad thing. A lot of manly men have them on their chins."

"You don't," C.J. pointed out. "Are you manly?"

There was amusement in Adam's gaze when he looked at her, but Jill felt her cheeks burn. She could vouch for his manliness. She had firsthand experience with it, or rather her mouth did.

Adam laughed. "I guess I'm just not one of the lucky guys."

C.J. squirmed on the exam table. "It hurts to get stitches."

"I have to give you some medicine with a little tiny needle, so it doesn't hurt while I'm putting them in. That will be like a pinch but it'll go away pretty fast. Then we'll wait till it works and you need to hold really still while I fix it up. Afterward it will ache, but not too bad."

"I don't know if I can hold still."

"I'll make a deal," Adam said. "If you hold as still as you can, I'll take you out to dinner. Anywhere you want to go."

"Really?"

"I promise." Adam held up his hand, palm out.

C.J. didn't look at her for an okay. Adam had put him in control and this was a man-to-man deal. Finally he nodded and said, "Okay. I'll be so still I won't even breathe."

"Breathing is okay." Adam laughed. "If it hurts more than I said, I'll even buy you ice cream after dinner."

"Cool."

Then Adam did exactly what he said and C.J. was calm and quiet because he hadn't been lied to. There were no surprises and he'd been well prepared for what was going to happen. He held still, didn't cry and actually gave the doctor a hug when it was all over. Jill was grateful to Adam, but that was the easy part. Everything else was incredibly complicated.

Not only was Dr. Stone easy on the eyes, he was good with kids. Also good with mothers, Jill thought. The man was a double threat. She needed that like she needed a sharp stick in the eye.

It got too late last night for dinner out after Adam stitched up C.J.'s chin. For all his talk about the cool factor of scars, he'd worked hard and taken his time putting in the tiniest stitches possible to minimize any mark the repair would leave. How was a mom supposed to resist a guy like that? It was the reason she kept her inner skeptic on high alert, although Jill conceded, if only to herself, that it was handy to have a doctor in the house. Technically not *in,* but just upstairs was close enough.

This morning before heading to the clinic, Doctor Dashing had stopped by to inspect the injury for infection and ask about pain. Both were a negative. Then he'd mentioned his promise and asked if it was okay to take C.J. to dinner that night. How could she object to a man who kept a promise?

Adam had come home from the clinic about fifteen minutes ago. She knew that because C.J. had been waiting and looking out the window. When he spotted the doctor's car in the driveway, her son had made the announcement at the top of his lungs and in a pitch only dogs could hear. Now he was getting ready to go out.

She was happy her little wounded soldier wasn't disappointed this time, but disillusionment was coming. Maybe not tonight or tomorrow, but sooner or later her little guy was going to get his heart stomped on and crushed when Adam decided his wilderness experiment wasn't the rollicking good time he'd expected and left Blackwater Lake. There was no way to prepare C.J. for that.

"How do I look, Mom?"

Jill glanced away from the computer screen she hadn't really been looking at anyway. C.J. stood beside her desk in his navy blue Sunday pants and long-sleeved yellow checked shirt. He was wearing sneakers because that was his only pair of shoes. Church and Sunday school were once a week, but his feet grew every day. Shoes got too small too fast and were too expensive for a dress-up pair. She figured God didn't mind a boy wearing sneakers instead of dress shoes as long as they walked into His house.

Her son's wavy red hair was slicked down with what looked like a *very* generous amount of gel. And water. Drops of it glistened on his forehead. Waiting for her approval, he was almost as still as he'd been last night while Adam had gently and skillfully closed the gash on his chin. The only evidence of yesterday's trauma was a small white bandage.

"Earth to Mom—"

She should get used to hearing her own words tossed back at her. This was another of many signs that he was growing up far too fast, and unshed tears burned her eyes. She was able to hold them back and chalked one up for Mom.

"You look more handsome than usual tonight," she said. "It must be the manly scar on your chin. Does it hurt?"

"Nah. Dr. Adam was wrong about that. It doesn't ache at all."

Just then there was a knock on the door. Speaking of the devil...

C.J. ran to answer it. "Hi, Dr. Adam."

"Hi, champ." He smiled when she moved behind her son. "Hello, mother of champ."

Jill wasn't sure how he managed to look better every time she saw him, but it was a fact. In his battered brown leather jacket and jeans that were worn almost white in the most interesting places, he had the rugged appearance every woman expected of a Montana man. Maybe that was why she felt a constant need to remind him he wasn't from there.

"Hi, Adam." Her voice had a breathless quality that she couldn't seem to control. "C.J. was just saying that you were wrong."

"Really?" He looked down. "About what?"

"My chin didn't hurt at all after you got done fixin' it. And it doesn't ache now."

"That's a very good thing to be wrong about."

Jill couldn't agree more. "He's doing great, Adam. You were so good with him. And now taking him to dinner— I can't thank you enough."

"Don't mention it." He looked at the little guy and whistled. "You look spiffy."

"Is that good?"

"Yes." Adam's expression was wry when he met her gaze. "I feel officially old now."

Jill laughed. "Then you won't be keeping him out too late. An old guy like you should be able to get him home in time for bed."

"Not a problem."

His blue eyes sparkled with something that made Jill's pulse stutter. Somehow she knew the deceptively simple word *bed* was making him think about that complicated kiss. God knew memories of it were never far from her mind, but she had high hopes of them fading very soon.

"Take good care of him—" Jill pressed her lips together. "Sorry. I'm sure you will. That's just automatic."

"I understand. It's a mom thing." He snapped his fingers as if an idea just occurred to him. "You should come with us."

"Oh, no. I couldn't." She looked down at her own jeans, worn all day at the marina, and seized on that as an excuse. "I'm not dressed for it."

"You can change. We'll wait, right, C.J.?"

Her son rubbed a finger beneath his nose. "Do we hafta?"

"No." Adam folded his arms over his chest. "But waiting for women is something we men do. It's probably time for you to start learning. I promise the wait is worth it."

"Now, there's something you're wrong about." Jill prayed that would discourage him. There was a very real possibility that her resolve to resist him was no match for that roguish sparkle in his eyes. "You and C.J. go on. There's a microwave dinner with my name on it in the freezer."

"That's just too sad." Adam met her gaze, and his own was potent with challenge. "Are you afraid to go?"

C.J. studied her. "It's the Grizzly Bear Diner, Mom. And the ones they got there are just stuffed."

"Like you are after eating there." She started to ruffle his hair, then remembered his effort to tame his curls. "Thanks for the support, sweetie."

"Does that mean you're comin' with us?" he asked impatiently.

"Yeah," Adam said. "Are you?"

Jill wasn't sure whether it was the sparkle in his eyes or the charming grin, but her resistance to the invitation was a miserable failure. "It will just take me a couple of minutes to change."

In her room Jill slipped into a pair of dark slacks and pulled a black-and-white sweater over her head. She twisted her hair into a knot and secured it with a clip, lifting some curls for height at her crown. Then she brushed some blush on her cheeks and smoothed tinted gloss over her lips.

Adam whistled when he saw her. "That wasn't much of a wait, but definitely worth it."

"Can we go now?" C.J. looked up at them. "I'm really starvin'."

"Me, too." A huskiness crept into the doctor's voice that hinted at exactly what he was hungry for and it had nothing to do with food.

Heart pounding, Jill got her son into his jacket and the three of them out the door in record time. Fifteen minutes later they were sitting in a booth at the grizzly bear–themed diner with C.J. next to Adam and the two of them across the table from her. She wasn't sure if a full-on view of the doctor was less dangerous than being on the same side and brushing arms, but that was the way it worked out. The Grizzly had a pretty decent crowd for a weeknight and she knew practically everyone here. They all stared at Adam as if the enemy had waltzed into their territory and taken it without a shot being fired.

Before they had their jackets off, Harriet Marlow, the owner of the diner, walked over with three glasses of water and set them down on the table. The blonde, who was some-where in her forties and what people diplomatically called "fluffy," had twenty extra pounds, which were her own best advertisement for the food she served in her establishment.

"Hey, Jill, haven't seen you in here for a while."

"Hi, Harriet." She silently pleaded that her son wouldn't share the reason why it had been so long was financial. "I've been busy."

Harriet studied the man across from her. "You must be the new doctor here in town."

"Adam Stone." He smiled as if the mistrust in her eyes wasn't there.

"He put stitches in my chin 'cuz I fell and hurt it. Wanna see?" C.J. offered.

"Maybe later."

"He said if I held really still while he did it, I could have dinner out wherever I wanted. I didn't move even once."

"Good for you, big guy."

"And I wanted to come here. I really like the bear paw burger and fries."

"As I recall, you get that with cheese," Harriet said, pull-ing a pencil and pad from her apron pocket.

"Yes, ma'am." C.J. grinned. "And I'd like a Coke."

"Sorry, kiddo," Jill cut in. "I know you were promised whatever you wanted, but I have to rule out anything with caffeine."

"O-okay," he said grudgingly. "Then lemonade."

"Coming right up." The plump woman smiled for the first time and almost included Adam. "Do you two need a min-ute?"

"I do." Jill always savored the luxury of a dinner she didn't have to prepare by looking at all the choices on the menu. But meals out were so rare, her usual burger would be the selection just because she knew she liked it and wouldn't be let down.

"Since this is my first time, I'll need to check it all out," Adam said.

"I'll give you a few minutes. Nice to see you, Jill."

"You, too, Harriet." She reached for two menus stacked behind the napkin holder and condiment containers, then handed one across to Adam.

As they were flipping through, Mayor Goodson stopped by the table. She smiled at C.J. "I heard about your adventure at the clinic yesterday."

"I bleeded a lot," he confirmed eagerly. Now that the pain and suffering were over, the story would take on a legend of its own. "Wanna see my stitches?"

"No, I'm sure Dr. Stone did a fine job."

"Took him forever," C.J. groaned. "I thought he'd never be done, but I didn't move. Not even my eyes. I just closed 'em."

"It's true," Adam agreed. "He was very manly."

"And I'm gonna have a big scar."

"He was very brave," Jill added. "And Adam was kind enough to reward him with dinner here because he was so good."

"That's the spirit, Doc." The mayor nodded her approval. "I hear we're going to see you at the Harvest Festival."

"I'm all signed up."

"Good." Loretta lifted a hand to wave goodbye. "Gotta run. See you there."

"She's stopping at every table," Adam commented.

Jill glanced over her shoulder and noticed that the people talking to the mayor were looking in this direction and the hostility level had gone down several notches. "I think Mayor Goodson is spreading the news of your good deed."

"I didn't put her up to it," Adam said quickly.

"That actually never crossed my mind. Because you didn't

know this place would be C.J.'s choice or that the mayor would be here."

"Wow." There was a teasing expression in his voice. "Good to know you trust me without any evidence to back it up."

"I trust you, too, Dr. Adam." C.J. was kneeling on the plastic booth bench, his elbows on the table. "Does it hurt to get stitches out? Can I keep 'em in forever?"

"They can't stay in more than a week." Adam thought for a moment. "It doesn't hurt, but you'll feel a little pulling. I'll do it really fast."

"Okay." There was no sign of apprehension as he blew on the straw in his water glass. He had complete faith in this man.

As it turned out, a full-on view of Adam wasn't the most dangerous thing that night. It was the hero worship in her son's eyes. It was seeing him so happy to be hanging around with another guy, the three of them having fun. This outing was a glimpse of what being a family was like. She'd experienced it a long time ago, before her father walked out, but C.J. never had. The yearning to give it to him welled up inside her.

Why did Adam have to be the one she pictured a family with? That was just crazy, especially when he'd flat out told her he wasn't interested. If she knew how to get the thought out of her head, Jill would do it in a heartbeat. Holding out hope for something like that with Adam Stone was just asking for trouble. If life had taught her anything, it was that she didn't have to ask for trouble.

It had a way of finding her on its own.

Chapter Seven

When Adam had made the decision to move to Montana, it never crossed his mind that he'd be the man voted most likely to be hate-stared out of town. In his medical station at the annual Harvest Festival he felt the vibe in a more public way than ever before. Folks walked by and looked at him as if an alien would burst out of his chest.

So far he had a boyhood friend and a six-year-old boy in the friends column. Mayor Goodson was civil to him mostly because she was a civil servant and it was literally in her job description. So here he sat by himself trying to rally some character and not let the isolation bother him, but that was hard for a guy who'd been popular in high school and college. Even in med school and afterward, people had accepted him easily. Shoot, he was an easygoing and likable guy—everywhere but Blackwater Lake.

Cars had been detoured off Main Street to close it off for the festival, and the booths were set up in the road. All the retail stores were open and hoping to take advantage of foot traffic.

Adam was situated between the Chamber of Commerce and Tourism booths. Behind him there was a big sign in blue letters advertising Mercy Medical Clinic health screenings. He'd been there since 10:00 a.m. and it was now past one. A handful of people who probably weren't Jill's friends had stopped by for blood pressure screenings, flu shots and cholesterol checks. The stack of brochures regarding healthy lifestyles and warning signals for stroke had hardly gone down at all.

Mostly he was doing nothing except fielding hostile looks from the residents of Blackwater Lake and really starting to resent taking the heat for "the last doctor" who had done Jill wrong. He was beginning to wonder if folks would ever give him a chance. At this point convincing them he was different looked doubtful.

Cabot Dixon separated from the people meandering down the street and walked over. He was carrying Tyler, who had his head on his father's shoulder. "How's it going?"

"Quiet. Not much has changed since the last time I saw you at the clinic."

That wasn't completely true. He'd kissed Jill, but it seemed that would stay between the two of them. If she'd mentioned anything, a lynch mob would have come after him with a whole lot to say before hanging him from the highest tree. Since he was still getting the silent treatment, the obvious conclusion was that no one else knew. Looking at it that way, he was doing all right.

"Give it time," his friend said.

"I'm a doctor. That's my line."

Cabot shrugged. "Apparently it's universal advice."

"Maybe, but at this rate I'll be retired before there's a

crack in the attitude." He folded his arms over his chest. "Hey, Tyler."

"Hi." He didn't lift his head, which was uncharacteristic of a six-year-old boy.

"You feeling okay?" Adam asked.

"He went on the roller coaster and Ferris wheel back-to-back. That was a couple of twists, rolls and turns too many after a hot dog and cotton candy. My fault." There was a dark look in Cab's eyes, something that said he blamed himself for a lot. "I'm taking him home."

"Wish I could go with you," Adam said.

"How long are you here at the festival?" Cabot asked.

"The booth is open till four. Although I'm on call for the clinic, too."

"Something tells me you're hoping to hear from the answering service."

Adam shrugged. "It would break up the monotony."

"Hang in there," the other man advised.

"Daddy, my tummy hurts," Tyler groaned. "Can we go home now?"

"Yeah, buddy. I'll get you there soon." He looked at Adam. "Any advice for a stomachache, Doc?"

"Time."

Cabot smiled ruefully. "See you later."

"Yeah. Feel better, Tyler."

Adam watched father and son move quickly away in the direction of the temporary lot at the edge of town set up for public parking. He looked at his watch and noted the friendly interlude had lasted the better part of five minutes. It was a nice break.

He could use more of them. And that's when he saw a familiar redhead in the flow of people walking by. Jill. A feeling of profound lust poured through him. He wanted her so bad he could taste it. Just from one look. It was a damn good thing he didn't see her every day. When his vision cleared and the blood started circulating back to his brain, he noticed that C.J. was beside her.

The kid glanced around and spotted Adam, then ran toward him, grinning. "Hi, Dr. Adam."

"Hey, champ. It's good to see you." A smiling face in this town was priceless. "Are you having fun?"

"Sort of."

Jill followed her son. She wasn't smiling, but she didn't look like she wanted him lynched either. "Hi."

"What are you up to?"

"Not much," she answered.

"That would explain the 'sort of' response to having fun." At the sight of her, Adam's spirits rose in a very different way from talking with Cabot.

"No, the explanation for that is his friend Tyler got a tummy ache and had to go home."

"Tyler and me were s'posed to ride *all* the rides and then go to the baseball booth. The one where you knock the bottles down and win somethin'. I been practicin'. I coulda won a really good prize."

"You can still go," his mother pointed out.

"It's no fun by myself."

"What am I, chopped liver?" she protested.

He plopped his tush down on the folding chair set up for patients. "You're a girl."

Not new information, Adam thought. The slender legs and curvy curves were a giveaway. And, after more clinical evaluation in the weeks since he'd been there, his assessment of her excellent derriere hadn't changed. It was still in the top five, although he was leaning toward a number one ranking now.

"Sorry, kiddo." Jill sighed. "I'm sure Tyler doesn't like not feeling well even more than you miss him being here."

"What's this thing?" He picked up the cuff with the attached bulb to inflate it.

Adam squatted down in front of him. "That's a blood pressure cuff."

"What's it for?"

"Taking people's blood pressure." Adam knew what was coming. "It goes on your arm and measures the force of blood pushing against the walls of your arteries. If the needle on the gauge reads too high, that means the blood is moving at a pressure not within normal range. That could be dangerous."

"Can you take mine?" Pleading brown eyes blinked at him.

"This one's too big for you. It's for grown-ups."

"Oh, man." C.J.'s posture was pure dejection. "I can't do anything. I wish you could go with me to the baseball booth."

Adam wasn't quite sure how the two thoughts connected, but the meaning of both was clear. "Me, too. But I can't leave here for a while."

"Why not?" The boy looked around. "There's no one here."

"Someone might come by," he explained. Although the odds weren't good on that. "High blood pressure screening is really important because there are no warnings if you have it."

"No tummy ache?" he asked.

"Nope. So, just in case, I need to be here."

"Dr. Adam is checking other things, too," Jill explained. "And giving flu shots for anyone who needs one."

"I don't," the boy said. "I don't like needles."

"I remember." Adam smiled as he inspected the red line under the small chin. He'd taken the stitches out a few weeks ago. There'd been no drama or tears, which could mean the kid trusted him more after dinner out. He'd really enjoyed spending time with the two of them. "That's a good-looking scar."

"It's hardly noticeable," Jill said. "You did an amazing job."

He smiled at her. "Happy to help."

"Can't someone take your place here?" C.J. persisted.

"Sorry, champ. I gave my word."

"What does that mean?"

"I promised and have to follow through. It's a responsibility."

Jill looked at her watch. "Have you had lunch?"

"No."

"You must be starving." There was concern in her voice.

"I'm okay."

"C.J. and I can get you something," she offered.

It surprised and pleased him that she'd go out of her way. Just talking about eating had his stomach rumbling, especially with all the food smells in the air. "Is someone selling pizza?"

"By the slice," she confirmed.

C.J. pointed. "Just down there."

"Tell me what you want."

"Let me go, Mommy." C.J. slid off the chair. "You can watch me. I wanna do it for Dr. Adam. He might get cranky if his sugar gets low."

Her smile was sheepish. "Can you tell we've talked about that?"

"Figured."

There was uncertainty in Jill's eyes. "I don't know, sweetie. Why don't we go together?"

"She never lets me do anything by myself," he grumbled to Adam. "Even though I'm gettin' bigger every day."

The "she" in question chewed on her bottom lip, clearly

conflicted. "You're right, C.J. You are a big boy. And I can see you from right here."

He looked up at Adam. "What kind do you want?"

"Pepperoni." Adam reached into his pocket and pulled out a twenty-dollar bill, then handed it over. "And a bottle of water. Can you carry all that?"

"'Course I can."

"Get something for yourself, too."

"Nah. I don't wanna get sick like Ty." He took the money and raced to the booth where the pizza was.

Adam watched him. "That hair makes him easy to spot."

The color was identical to Jill's. He studied her, never looking away from her son. She was definitely not hard on the eyes and he felt the wanting well up the way it always did when she was near. If she was just beautiful, the knot in his gut wouldn't be so bad. He'd met a lot of beautiful women who didn't get to him, but there was something about this woman that did. Unfortunately acting on the attraction complicated everything he was trying to accomplish.

"Hi, Jill." A tiny, gray-haired woman stopped.

"Mrs. Carberry. I haven't seen you in ages. How are you?"

"Pretty well." She glanced at Adam. "You're the new doctor?"

"Yes, ma'am."

"He's doing free blood pressure checks, among other things," Jill said. "You should do it."

"Really?"

"I promise it won't hurt," Adam said. "Unless you want a flu shot, but that's only a little stick. I recommend it. Risk factors are higher in your age demographic."

"Are you saying I'm old?" she demanded, although there was a twinkle in her blue eyes.

"No." He shook his head. "I just meant—"

The woman grinned and sat in the folding chair. "Just messing with you, Doc. If Jill thinks I should, then I will."

Adam did his thing and Mrs. Carberry decided to get the shot because she'd had a bad case of flu the year before. As he worked, he noticed a few more people chatting with Jill. She was pointing in his direction and it looked as though a small line was forming. Maybe the town sweetheart was starting to like him and would pass along the sentiment to her friends and neighbors.

That would help his cause, if he could only forget how good it had felt to kiss that hometown sweetheart. If only he could unkiss her, because the memory was powerful and just made him want her more. The temptation was damned inconvenient, especially with the thaw in her attitude. Because he didn't have the aptitude to do it right, pursuing a relationship with Jill Beck would be a big mistake.

Based on the Blackwater Lake cold shoulder he'd already experienced, if he screwed it up, acceptance in this town would be next to impossible.

Jill rubbed her eyes and then glanced at her watch, surprised at the time. It was Saturday, but unlike most people she wasn't off. She'd been at the computer for several hours, still making up for the half a day she'd squeezed out of her schedule for the Harvest Festival a week ago. First she'd completed an assignment for an online class, then her own budget. Adam Stone's rent check had cleared and it hit her that he'd been upstairs for two months now. Since renters paid ahead, he was going on number three.

When they'd first met, the weather had been sunny and warm, one of those perfect Montana days that made you forget the awful ones. And the awful ones were coming soon. Last night on the news the anchor had warned that a cold front was coming.

She stood and pressed her hands to her back, then raised her arms over her head and stretched from side to side. C.J. had been at the marina store with Brew all afternoon. It was almost time for dinner and she decided to walk down to get him. A phone call would do the job, but she needed some exercise after sitting for so long. Grabbing her quilted jacket from the hall tree, she opened the front door and gasped. The glare had her shielding her eyes.

"Snow."

Normally the first storm of the season was exciting, but not this one. A vague sensation of depression settled over her.

Footsteps sounded on the stairway to the upstairs apartment and moments later Adam appeared at the bottom. The last time they'd seen each other was when he'd given Mrs. Carberry a flu shot. Somehow, maybe by unspoken mutual agreement, they steered clear of meeting like this and she wasn't used to bumping into him. That was definitely for the best since she knew he was the reason for her lack of first snowfall joy. This was the kind of weather that would send a doctor from Dallas back to his warmer natural habitat.

"It's snowing." He was just shrugging into his jacket.

"The weather guy said it was a possibility, but I figured he was wrong. It's early." And just this once she'd so hoped winter would hold off. "You've been keeping long hours at the clinic."

"I've been pretty busy. Thanks to you." He slid his hands into the pockets of his sheepskin-lined jacket. "Haven't even had a chance to thank you for not only acknowledging me in public, but giving a recommendation, too."

"You're a good doctor, Adam. And definitely C.J.'s hero. Not only did you convince my son the wiggle worm to hold still, but the care you took closing up that nasty gash on his chin was amazing."

"I'd have turned C.J. over to someone in plastics if they were close by."

Jill had considered trekking to the hospital, but that was about her personal reasons for avoiding Adam. "I can't imagine a plastic surgeon doing a better job."

"A specialist knows the latest and best techniques in the field so patients get the most positive outcome possible." He blew out a breath, and a white cloud appeared in front of his face. "Family practice physicians see anyone with any problem and become experts in common problems. With C.J., I just used the smallest sutures available and put in as many as possible to minimize scarring."

"Clearly you've patched up little boys before." She rocked back on her heels.

"Accidents happen to everyone, all ages. I treated a grown woman who decided to go after an avocado pit with the business end of her paring knife. The pit shifted and the point of the blade went straight into her palm."

"Ouch." Jill winced.

"I'm told it wasn't painful in spite of the blood splatter. But her husband was kind of freaked out."

"That doesn't surprise me." She smiled at him and he smiled back. It was too nice and to break the spell she glanced away. "Boy, the snow is coming down even harder now. At this rate, the roads could be a problem."

"Yeah." His expression turned grim.

"What's wrong?"

"Mommy, look!" C.J. came running up the front walk. "It's snowing."

"I see that," she said.

"Hey, Dr. Adam, wanna have a snowball fight?"

The doctor smiled and ruffled the red hair. "Wish I could, champ, but—"

"Hey, Jill." Brewster was hurrying up the front path. The

walkway was now covered with snow and only someone familiar with the property would know where it was. Although her son's small footprints were still there, they were quickly being obscured. "It's comin' down hard."

"Yeah." What was it about the first snow that made everyone, including her, state the obvious?

Brewster stepped on the porch and stomped his feet. "If it's all the same to you, I'd like to head out before I get stuck here. You know how Hildie worries about her man."

"I do. Definitely go home," she said.

"Thanks." He looked at Adam. A friendly look that was new and different. "Hi, Doc."

"Mr. Smith."

Brew held out his hand. "Wanted to say thanks."

"For what?" Adam squeezed the other man's palm.

"I don't know what kind of medicine you gave my wife, but she's a new woman." He rubbed his chin. "It's more like she's back to her old self. Only better."

"I'm glad to hear it."

There was a twinkle in Brewster's blue eyes. "She's frisky again, if you know what I mean."

"I don't know," C.J. said. "What do you mean?"

"Just that," Jill interrupted, "Hildie has more energy. Right, Dr. Adam?"

"That's right." His grin was the epitome of male satisfaction. "More energy."

"And how." The older man grinned. "Doc, let me know if you decide you want that boat finished. It's the least I can do."

"I will, Mr. Smith—"

"Call me Brew." He turned and headed for the steps. With a wave, he said, "Talk to you tomorrow, Jill."

"Okay." Bewildered, she met Adam's gaze. "I think I just witnessed a miracle."

"What?" Adam said.

"Don't pretend you don't know. Brewster was nice to you."

"I got that. I'm pretty observant. I tend to notice when someone isn't trying to rip my head off."

"Brew tried to do that?" C.J. said, bewildered in his six-year-old way.

"Not recently," Adam clarified.

"What did you give Hildie?" Jill asked.

"I could tell you, but then I'd have to kill you. That's just a funny grown-up expression, champ," he explained to the boy. "Patient privacy laws are carved in stone—no pun intended." The cell phone in the case hooked to his belt vibrated and he plucked it out and answered, "Stone." He listened and his expression grew serious. "I'll meet you at the clinic. Be careful, Brady."

"Brady O'Keefe?" Jill took a wild guess and Adam's nod confirmed it.

"Maggie's in labor. He called me earlier and said he was taking her to the hospital. In case he couldn't get through because of the storm, he wanted to give me a heads-up."

"So, you're going to deliver her baby." It wasn't a question. He was the only doctor around.

"Yeah."

"Is her mom with her? Maureen is her birth coach."

"Brady didn't say. But don't worry. Delivering babies is another one of those common problems we family doctors face every day. And first babies, like all of them, are notoriously unpredictable. I have to run." He smiled at C.J. "We'll have that snowball fight another time."

"Okay."

"Bye." He waved, then jogged down the steps and turned left toward his car.

Jill watched the big, fat flakes falling out of the gray sky quickly start to obscure his footprints in the snow. Hildie wasn't the only one worried about her man out in the snow.

But Adam wasn't Jill's man. She didn't have the right to worry about him.

Did he know how to drive in snow? Did he have chains? Four-wheel drive? What if he had an accident? Would anyone notify her?

She didn't like this thought process one single bit but couldn't seem to turn it off. Fretting wasn't something you did for just anyone. It was something you did for someone you had feelings for. She didn't want to have feelings for Adam. Especially not now.

She looked up at the snow falling and sighed. An early winter just meant he'd skip out that much sooner. It was impossible to ignore how sad her heart was at the thought of him not in the apartment upstairs.

Chapter Eight

Jill woke early the next morning tired and crabby. She hadn't slept well, which was unusual for her during a snowstorm. The falling flakes always made everything especially hushed and still. It felt as if Mother Nature tucked the world in for a nap. Outside, everything was quiet and serene, but apparently not inside, at least for her. She couldn't stop herself from worrying about Adam driving in bad weather. And her friend Maggie was giving birth without the baby's father, the love of her life, by her side. Nothing was right and Jill felt helpless.

At least C.J. wasn't stirring yet. It was Sunday and he didn't have to get up for school. She hoped he would sleep in for a while.

She got up and dressed in warm clothes—jeans, sweater, boots—then went to the kitchen for coffee. Grounds and water were ready, but she was up before the automatic timer was set to go off. She hit the on button and soon heard the hiss and sizzle of the water followed by the warm, rich smell of her morning pick-me-up. Normally the familiar routine made her happy. There was comfort and stability in sameness, but nothing had been the same since Adam Stone had showed up in her life.

He hadn't returned before she went to bed last night and she'd stayed awake listening for the sound of his car. Sometime during the night she fell asleep and didn't know if he'd come home or not. Had he made it to the clinic? Were the roads passable? And if not, what happened to Maggie? She didn't like this at all. She didn't like that he was important enough for her to actively worry about. It wasn't the general concern of one human being for another. This was more, and scary.

She poured herself a cup of coffee, then went to the living room window to check out the driveway for his car. Her inspection never made it past the front walk where Adam was shoveling snow. Her snow, from her front walk.

The surge of joy coursing through her was a dangerous thing and she knew it, but there was no controlling something with a life of its own. If she were smart, she'd turn around, go to the computer and use this quiet time for her online econ class. It seemed she wasn't very bright because she poured coffee into a second mug, put on her jacket and gloves, then went outside and stood on the porch.

He was facing away and apparently hadn't heard her because the shoveling continued. He kept moving the snow from her walkway to the growing white pile beside it. The first rays of sun were just peeking over the top of the mountains and gave her more light to admire the broad expanse of his shoulders that made this tedious job far easier for him than it would be for her. His jacket hung over the porch railing and he was wearing jeans and a navy-and-brown plaid flannel shirt. The look was very geek-meets-lumberjack and worked for her in a very big, very unsettling way.

"Good morning," she said, her voice sounding louder in the early stillness. She started down the steps toward him.

He turned and spotted her with the coffee. It wasn't clear if one or both were responsible for the wide smile. "Hi."

She handed him the still-steaming mug. "I wasn't sure whether you like it black or not. There's milk and sugar inside."

"This is fine." He took a sip and his face registered sheer pleasure. "Better than fine."

"You're up early."

"Actually, I never went to bed. Just got home a little while ago."

Maybe the sound of his car had awakened her so early, possibly because on a subconscious level she'd been listening for him. Then she remembered why he'd been up all night. What with checking him out in detail, she'd forgotten about the reason he'd rushed off to the clinic—was it really yesterday?

"How's Maggie?" she asked.

"She's the proud mother of a beautiful, healthy baby girl— seven pounds, four ounces, twenty inches long."

"Danielle Maureen," Jill whispered, knowing the child would have been named after her father. "Maggie and Danny chose not to find out the sex of the baby, but he wanted a girl who looks just like her mother. That's the name they picked out."

Adam's brooding expression indicated that his thoughts turned a little sad. "It's hard to tell just yet who she looks like, but Danny got his little girl."

"I'm glad you were here to help her into the world."

"Me, too." He jammed the shovel into the snow, then went to sit on the top porch step, holding the mug between his palms. When she sat beside him, he said with a touch of awe and pride, "I just delivered my first Blackwater Lake baby."

First, as in he would be bringing more babies into this town, which meant he was planning to stay.

Happiness bubbled up inside her. "I think Maggie's baby should get some kind of award."

Adam looked sideways at her. "Do you, now?"

"Seems fair." She shrugged. "A blue ribbon—maybe pink, considering she's a girl."

"I can do better than a prize. I'm going to set up a college fund for her and make the first contribution."

Jill's heart melted like snow in the sun. "That's very thoughtful."

"It's only right. Her father gave his life for this country. The least I can do is make an investment in a good life for his daughter."

Jill couldn't think of a way to express how sweet this gesture was, and that was just as well. She had a lump in her throat the size of Montana and couldn't get words past it.

She swallowed hard. "I'm surprised Brady didn't call me about the baby," she said instead.

"He and Maureen talked about the list of people to notify, but there was a lot to do first what with getting mother and baby settled at home."

"She doesn't need to be in the hospital?" Jill asked.

"No. Everything about the birth was textbook normal and the baby's Apgar—the score for evaluating newborns," he explained, "was right on target. Virginia, my nurse, is going to check in on mother and baby. Of course I'm on call. After all that, they decided to wait for morning to make calls," he finished.

"That makes sense. Everyone is fine. That's most important." She looked at him and then the snow shovel. "And you're still here." She hadn't meant to lump that in the "most important" category, but somehow it came out that way. "Shoveling snow on my walkway."

"I am." He took a sip of coffee. "For the record, I wouldn't have been able to pull off a clandestine getaway since there's an apartment up there with a lot of stuff in it. But the point is that I'm not going anywhere. Talk is cheap. The best way to prove I'm not afraid of a little cold weather is to embrace it."

"Put your money where your mouth is? So to speak," she added.

"Exactly." He rubbed the back of his neck. "If I were a mean-spirited sort of person, I'd have you take a picture of me with the snow shovel and text it to my mother."

"Cell service is spotty here in the mountains, and why would you want to?"

"As a giant 'take that,'" he admitted. "I've been getting pressure from the home front."

She finished the last of the cold coffee in her mug, then asked, "About what?"

"Going home."

"To Dallas?"

"Yeah." He looked at her. "Mom called when she heard about the storm on the news. She wanted to know if I'm finished playing country doctor yet. Was I cold and ready to end this back-to-nature experiment? Did I miss the Dallas Metroplex where it's flat and the sun is shining on roads not covered with snow?"

"And?"

"No."

"No, what?" she nudged.

"I don't miss Texas. I like the mountains and the cold. Shoveling snow is good exercise and I'm staying put." He grinned. "The text picture would be me letting my actions speak louder than words my mother refuses to hear."

"I think your mother's reaction is understandable."

The surprise on his face said that wasn't what he'd expected from her. "*Understandable* isn't a word I normally hear coming out of your mouth."

"I deserve that. I've been skeptical about your longevity here in Blackwater Lake."

"You and everyone else," he added wryly.

Jill ignored that. "But this is your mother we're talking about. Of course she'd like her son to be close by. God knows if it were C.J., I'd want him under my roof forever."

"Trust me on this. No guy wants to live with his mother, and if he does, serious therapy should be considered, stat." He rested his forearms on his knees. "Don't get me wrong. I love my folks. And I plan to visit them. But the life they made for themselves isn't the one I want for me."

Jill smiled. "Then I'm sure your family is pleased that you have it. From the maternal perspective, I can say with absolute certainty that parents ultimately want their children to be happy. It's what I want for my son."

And just then the front door opened and the son in question raced outside. "It's all white out here!" he declared as if he were the only one who could see and the world needed a newsflash.

Jill couldn't help smiling at the fact that snow was one of the things that always rated an exclamation point from her little guy. "Want to shovel it?"

"I wanna have a snowball fight first." He ran down the porch steps and shoved his hands into the white stuff. After mounding the snow into a ball, he threw it at Adam and made a direct hit.

Brushing at the wetness on his face, the doctor pretended anger that fooled no one, least of all C.J. "I can't believe I practiced throwing a baseball with you. I taught you everything you know and this is the thanks I get?"

"I'm gettin' pretty good. Betcha can't hit me." C.J. stood there, making himself a target. He was goading Adam to play.

"I'll show you good." And just like that Adam took the bait. He set down his mug and in one athletic motion descended the stairs and reached down for a handful of snow. "It's every man for himself."

C.J. waved his hands. "Can't hit me!" Famous last words because the first shot hit him in the chest with a gentle splat. "Lucky shot. Betcha can't hit me again."

But he didn't stand still and Adam chased him. This went on for a while and Jill couldn't figure out where Adam got the energy after being up all night. Then things shifted. Apparently there was unspoken male communication and they both turned on her, dragging her into the fray. After that it was a free-for-all. There was running, laughing, ducking around the house and behind bushes. Adam grabbed up C.J. and tickled him, making him squeal with laughter. Snowballs were flying and the spirit of revenge filled the air.

Ten minutes later they were all wet, cold and laughing. Jill hadn't had such carefree fun for longer than she could remember, but all good things must come to an end. "It's time to go inside."

"Aw, Mom. I want to play with Dr. Adam some more."

"Adam needs some sleep. He was up all night delivering Aunt Maggie's baby girl."

C.J. looked unimpressed. "Tyler and me wanted a boy."

"Sorry. That doesn't change the fact that he needs to rest and you have to get out of those wet things before you get sick."

"Okay," the boy said, trudging reluctantly up the porch steps. "Bye, Dr. Adam."

"Bye." Adam pushed the wet hair off his forehead. "See you later, Jill."

"Yeah." After her son disappeared inside, she watched the doctor walk toward the stairs leading to the second floor-apartment. A thought flashed into her mind and out came the words. "Hey, Adam, want to have dinner with us tonight?"

He stopped and looked over his shoulder. "To what do I owe the invitation?"

"Let's call it a thank-you for shoveling snow."

"Okay, let's." But the intense look in his eyes called it something else entirely. "What time?"

"How about five-thirty?"

"I'll be there."

And she'd be waiting.

At five-twenty-five Adam stood on Jill's porch where light spilled from her front window. Inside, there was laughter, love and hugs—and somehow he felt as if he was on the out-side looking in, all of that happiness just out of his reach. It was as if his nose was pressed up against the window and he was getting a glimpse of what he could never have. Being punished because he'd had his chance and blown it. Now he was a family practice doctor without a family.

The life I want for me.

He'd said that to Jill earlier but wasn't sure what that meant anymore. He hadn't thought past just wanting to move to Blackwater Lake, Montana. He loved the mountains, lake, outdoors. It was a place where he'd been happy. This proba-tion period the town put him through was unexpected. They had their reasons, and all of them were about Jill.

She was unexpected, too.

All this soul-searching, deep thought and questioning wasn't like him. Maybe he was overtired. Being up all night to deliver a baby could do that. The high of bringing a new life into the world had worn off. Even after sleeping for a few hours today, he couldn't seem to get it back. He couldn't shake the feeling that accepting this dinner invitation had been a bad idea, that no good would come of it. Just like the last time.

But he had accepted and not showing up would undo all the positive steps he'd taken. It was dinner with Jill and C.J. He would leave right after eating. What could happen?

After knocking he'd expected to hear the sound of six-year-old running feet. He didn't and was surprised when Jill answered.

"Hi. You're right on time."

"That happens when you don't have to worry about traffic on the drive over." He walked inside. "Where's C.J.?"

"Finishing up his shower. He didn't want to miss anything this time."

Adam remembered in vivid detail what the kid had missed last time. Heat poured through him at the memories of his mouth on Jill's, her soft body pressed against his. The feel of her in his arms was too perfect, but that was chemistry and physiology. Neither of those two things made the kiss right. He promised himself that there wouldn't be anything to miss tonight. It was just dinner. C.J. would be there. They'd eat, and then he would plead fatigue and go home. He would spread goodwill by keeping his word. Mission accomplished. End of story.

"It's cold out here." Jill rubbed her arms. "Come on in."

"Thanks."

He walked past her and looked around. The inside wasn't exactly as he remembered; Halloween decorations were everywhere. Fake webs hung on lamp shades, and picture frames had black plastic spiders stuck in them. Orange pumpkins of various sizes sat on flat surfaces throughout the living room. On Jill's desk was a stand about a foot high with hanging wooden cutouts of orange and white triangular candy corn, a witch's hat, ghosts and black bats.

"This looks very cool," he said.

"C.J. did a lot of it. I think he likes Halloween almost better than Christmas."

Adam could relate. But he didn't remember his house looking like this. His mother was too busy working. Except that excuse didn't quite cut it any more than he believed C.J. had done most of this. Jill worked, took classes online and was a single mom who found the time to decorate for a holiday.

Then he heard the sound of bare running feet slapping against the wooden floor just before the redheaded chaperone burst through the hall doorway.

"Hi, Dr. Adam."

"Hey, champ." He squatted down and the boy unexpectedly ran into his arms. The smell of freshly washed little boy slipped into a soft spot inside him. "You look clean."

"I am."

"Come on, you two. Dinner is ready." Jill walked toward the kitchen and glanced over her shoulder as she talked. "It's nothing fancy. Just homemade soup, salad and bread."

Adam followed, unable to resist a chance to appreciate the Beck backside at its best in a snug pair of jeans. "You baked bread?"

"I have a bread maker and a mix. Not a big deal."

"But it's not store-bought?" he clarified.

"No," she confirmed. "Soup is chicken and rice. C.J. and I like that when the weather turns cold."

"Mommy makes the best," her loyal son piped up.

"Sure smells good." Felt good. Too good. He took the same seat as last time and realized this was the beginning of a habit.

Jill put a tureen and ladle on the table, then pulled a bowl filled with greens from the refrigerator. After that she assembled the sliced homemade bread and butter and proceeded to toss the salad. "I hope you like oil and red wine vinegar."

"My favorite."

"Not mine." C.J. wrinkled his nose. "I don't like salad."

"Which is why you need to eat all the carrots in your soup." She sat down and gave her son a "mom" look. "I expect you to put some vegetables in your bowl along with the chicken and rice."

"Okay." The guilty expression was a clue that they'd been through this before.

After the boy was finished ladling, Adam helped himself. "Looks good."

"It's not mashed potatoes and hot dogs." Jill's eyes sparkled with mischief. "But it's filling."

Adam ate a spoonful and nodded appreciatively. It was hot, tasty and just the thing for a snowy evening. They ate in silence for a few moments before he asked, "So, C.J., what are you going to be for Halloween?"

"Maybe a doctor." He chewed on a carrot.

Jill looked uneasy as she warned, "That's not a for-sure."

A life lesson from mother to son, Adam thought. Never count on anything. Everyone learned it sooner or later. He'd gone into marriage thinking it would be forever and found out just how wrong he could be.

"Where do you go trick or treating?" he asked. "It's pretty isolated out here. The next house is a long way down the road."

Jill buttered a piece of bread. "I take C.J. into town and hit a few streets before the party at the town hall. The kids get the door-to-door experience in a safe environment."

"I can't imagine anything about Blackwater Lake being unsafe."

"True," she said. "We're lucky that way, but I don't take anything for granted."

"What are you gonna be, Dr. Adam?"

"I hadn't thought about it," he admitted. "I'll have to find out if the staff at the clinic dresses up." He grinned. "I can picture Virginia in a witch's hat, a big wart on her nose."

"Gives you a hard time, does she?" Jill's eyes twinkled.

"In a word? Yes." He shrugged. "There's no way to sugarcoat it."

Jill took a bite of her salad. "I don't know what I'd have done without Ginny when my mom got sick."

"She told me. I'm glad someone was there for you." He truly meant that.

"Mom, I'm finished with my soup. See?" He tilted his empty bowl for inspection.

"Good job, kiddo. All that outdoor activity must have made you hungry."

"I still am. Can I have dessert?"

"Yes. But you have to wait patiently until Adam and I are finished."

"Okay." The agreement was automatic, but actual compliance was like trying to hold back a tsunami after a magnitude-nine earthquake. He wiggled and watched, but there was nothing patient about his waiting. After a minute or two he asked, "Aren't you guys done yet?"

Jill met his gaze across the table as she scooped up the last of her soup.

"I'm finished. Adam?"

"Me, too." He tilted his empty bowl for them to see.

"Would you like more soup?" Clearly she enjoyed just the tiniest bit of teasing.

"He's full," C.J. said quickly. "Right, Dr. Adam?"

"Not quite." Adam couldn't resist a little ribbing of his own. But only a little. "I have just enough room left for dessert."

"Is it time now, Mom?"

"Yes." She smiled at her son, then said, "It's just ice cream."

"My favorite."

"Mine, too," the little guy added.

"I picked up a couple of quarts from Maggie's place. There was a picture of her and the baby up behind the cash register." She stood and carried her dishes to the sink.

"I'll get those." Adam stood and picked up the remaining plates, bowls and spoons.

"I wanna help." C.J. slid off his chair and followed Adam.

Jill pulled the ice cream out of the freezer, then scooped it into bowls and set them on the table. "Dig in, guys."

"Can I watch the movie about the toys while I eat my dessert? Please, Mommy. I won't spill."

She thought for a moment, but the soft look on her face wasn't leading up to a negative response. "Okay. Just this once."

"Can we all watch the movie?" C.J.'s expression was eager.

"Why not?"

So all of them trooped into the living room and Adam held her bowl while she put the DVD in the player and turned on the TV. The studio logo filled the screen, and the three of them sat on the sofa in front of it with the little boy in the middle. This scenario was not in Adam's frame of reference. A quiet night watching television and not being alone felt really nice, which was why he knew it was past time to leave. And he would, as soon as a decent amount of time passed so it didn't seem rude.

When they'd all finished their dessert, Jill took the empty bowls. "I'm just going to put everything in the dishwasher."

"Do you need some help?"

"No. Enjoy the movie." She smiled, then turned toward the kitchen.

He watched her walk away, the unconsciously sexy sway of her hips. Her curly hair spilled over the collar of her green sweater, and all he could think about was how beautiful she'd look naked, how much he wanted to see her thick red hair spread over a pillow. It was definitely time for him to say good-night.

About ten minutes later she was back, looking down at her son. "Someone's out cold."

"Not me." Adam was too hot to be cold, and that was all her fault. But that's not what she meant and she wasn't talking about him.

C.J. had curled against him, his head resting on Adam's chest. The slow, even breathing was a clue that the boy had fallen asleep.

She bent and tenderly brushed the hair off her son's forehead. "I guess he's worn out from all the activity today."

"Yeah."

With the sweet scent of her skin filling his head and her mouth so close, activities came to Adam's mind that were all about tangled legs and twisted sheets.

"He needs to be in bed," she said softly. "He's gotten so heavy it's not easy for me to pick him up. I'll try not to rouse him too much while I walk him to his room."

"I'll carry him in."

"That would be great. Thanks." Her gaze met his. "I'll turn down the bed."

He nodded, then picked up C.J., who mumbled something before curling into his chest. He was solid, all boy, and tugged at Adam's heart. This was just one more reason why coming tonight had been a boneheaded idea. But as soon as the kid was settled, he'd be out of there.

He followed Jill to the second bedroom and as gently as possible put the little guy on the superhero sheets. When C.J. turned on his side without waking, his mom pulled the matching comforter over him. After kissing the freckled cheek, she quietly walked out with Adam behind her.

In the living room, the movie was still softly playing. They stood by the back of the couch and looked at each other. Her eyes were liquid and soft and he could easily drown in them.

"I should go." Because he so badly wanted to stay.

"Yeah. You must be tired after pulling an all-nighter."

Not that tired, he thought, but kept the words inside. "I'm hanging in there."

She walked him to the door. "Thanks for shoveling my snow."

"You're welcome. Thanks for dinner." He put his hand on the knob and opened the door. Frigid air blew in and mixed with the seductive warmth of her. It took every ounce of his willpower to say, "Good night, Jill."

Adam looked down at her, the way she rubbed her arms against the cold, and couldn't make himself walk out. He wanted to keep her warm. He wanted to hold her.

He simply wanted her more than he'd wanted a woman in his life. When something in her eyes made him lean toward her, he lowered his head and she went up on tiptoe until their lips met.

No way was he leaving now.

Chapter Nine

The gentleness Adam had shown her son was Jill's undoing. The strong man, so careful with C.J., had made her all gooey and warm inside. How could a woman resist the sight of a strong man carrying a child, *her* child, with such obvious caring? And he'd shoveled her snow, for goodness' sake. The best she could do was soup and salad, but he'd been happy with that. She'd been fighting this overwhelming attraction since the first moment they'd met, and she just couldn't do it anymore. All of the above pushed her over the edge.

Their mouths touched and the contact unleashed everything she'd been holding back. She frantically tugged at the shirt tucked into his jeans. He groaned and settled his hands at her waist, sliding them under her sweater to touch her bare skin. His palms were warm and he moved them up slowly until his thumbs brushed the undersides of her breasts. She couldn't hold back a moan. It had been so long since she'd had a man's hands on her like this, she nearly wept from the sheer joy in the sensation.

When she undid the top button of his shirt and ran her finger over the dusting of hair in the V, he sucked in a quick breath and took her hand in his. He kissed each fingertip before drawing the index finger into his mouth and sucking deeply. She felt the pull all the way to her belly, and between her thighs an aching need started pulsing.

"I want you." Adam's eyes burned with intensity. "But not here."

"C.J.," she whispered.

He nodded and took her hand, tugging her down the hall, past where her son was sleeping and into the master bedroom. He closed and locked the door. Again her insides turned into melted goo at the sweet and considerate act.

The garage-sale bedside lamp with the scalloped, off-white shade was turned on, but Adam's tall form blocked the light. He took her closer to the bed, then stopped and cupped her face in his hands and kissed her. He tasted like chicken soup and ice cream, so ordinary—yet not. As kisses went, it was probably the best of her life. Not too slow or too fast. Not too hard or soft. Just the right amount of pressure to prime the passion. But she didn't need priming, she needed him.

Jill reached up and slid her finger over his earlobe, then down his neck and stopped at his collarbone. His groan of need at the lightest of touches made her smile and then he kissed it away. Tension arced between them and they pulled at each other's clothes again. Shirt and sweater came off and were tossed away. They worked the snaps and zippers on jeans and yanked them off, taking shoes and socks, too. The sound of their harsh breathing filled the room, but it was fueled by passion, not exertion.

She stood still while Adam reached around and undid the

clasp of her bra. The straps slid down her arms and he helped it along, his eyes intense and approving as he stared at her.

"You are so beautiful," he breathed, cupping her in his palms.

The feel of his hands on her bare flesh was too exquisite for words and she pressed herself more firmly against him. When he brushed his thumbs over her nipples, the sensation rocked her world and kicked her breathing up higher.

"That's so good," she whispered. "Too good."

She pulled away and yanked the throw pillows off the bed and pitched them over the other side onto the floor. Then she turned down the comforter and crawled onto the mattress before dragging the top sheet over her. Finally she wiggled out of her panties and tossed them on the floor.

Lifting herself up onto her forearm, she studied him, standing there in his boxers. He looked pretty spectacular. Wide shoulders, broad chest with just the right amount of hair, a flat belly and muscular legs. She judged him a fifteen on a scale of one to ten. And her gaze slid to that part of him that made him so male, so ready. It had been a long time for her. She was out of practice, not that she'd ever been in practice, and groaned as a thought struck her.

"What's wrong?"

She met his concerned gaze. "I don't have protection. Oh, Adam... This is awful. We can't... I can't..."

"I have a condom." He shrugged at her look. "I always have one. Don't leave home without it. Guy thing. Just don't read anything into it."

"Not judging, just grateful."

She watched the play of muscle on his back as he reached for his jeans, pulled out the wallet, then put the square packet on the nightstand.

Jill held out her arms and he dropped his boxers, and came to her in the bed. He pulled her against him and lowered them both to the mattress. He kissed her lips, her neck, her breasts, until she could hardly draw air into her lungs. She kissed him back, sliding her hands over his shoulders, arms and chest. They were touching everywhere except where she most wanted.

"Oh, God, Adam..."

"I know."

He rolled away and reached for the condom, then ripped it open. After covering himself, he pulled her back into his arms and shifted his body over hers. Taking his weight on his elbows, he entered her slowly, letting her body accept him. Moments later, he reached his hand between them to brush his thumb over the bundle of nerve endings at the juncture of her thighs. The touch was like a jolt from a live electrical wire that sent vibrations rippling through her, pleasure pulsing everywhere. She clung to him as her body shattered into a million pieces.

Breathing harsh and shallow, Adam thrust once more before he groaned and went still, then shuddered as he buried his face in her neck.

Jill wasn't sure how long they stayed like that or where Adam found the energy to move, but he did and went into the bathroom. The light went on and she heard water running. A few minutes later he was back and the mattress dipped from his weight as he slid back in bed and reached for her.

"That was really..." She stopped and sighed, unable to come up with a good enough adjective.

"I know." He linked her fingers with his, then rested their joined hands on his belly.

"This is nice." She yawned and snuggled against him.

There was something about a warm man beside you on a cold night. She missed it and sighed again as her eyes drifted closed. She must have slept because sometime during the night she woke up cold. Sliding her hand over, she searched for Adam, but he wasn't there. And the house was quiet. There were no unusual sounds suggesting he might still be around.

The disappointment of being alone was bigger and harder than she'd expected. Damn the cuddling. Sex was sex and it had been pretty fabulous, but holding each other after was intimate, and personal and really lovely. She hated the weakness, hated that she knew better but had ignored her own warnings.

Adam had left her bedroom door open and she heard C.J. call out in his sleep, probably a nightmare, which happened from time to time. Still naked, she slid out of bed and put on flannel pajamas. Maybe it was the cold air hitting her body, but common sense came back in a rush. What if C.J. had tried to come in and the door was locked? It never was and he'd have known something was up.

Her son badly wanted a man in his life, and finding his hero here would give him ideas. When it didn't work out the way he hoped, the fall would be even harder. As disappointed as she was, maybe it was for the best that Adam had left.

But, oh, how she wished his arms were still around her. The intensity of that feeling was a very scary thing.

Just before six in the evening Adam heard a knock on his door and the fact that it was Halloween gave him a big clue who was on the other side. He opened it and, as he'd thought, C.J. was there.

"Trick or treat!" The kid was wearing a small white coat with his name embroidered on the pocket, black horn-rimmed glasses and a plastic stethoscope around his neck.

"Hey, champ. You look like a doctor."

"I don't give shots," he said. "Mommy bought me a doctor set from the toy store with the thing that goes around your arm and a shot-giver, but I left that home."

"Good to know." He looked past the boy and saw Jill on the landing. "Hi."

She lifted a hand in greeting, then slid her fingers into the pockets of her jeans. It was possible for her to look more uncomfortable, but he wasn't sure how. He hadn't seen her since that mind-blowing night a couple of days ago. The look he saw on her face now said she was having second thoughts about sex.

Adam looked down at C.J. "I don't have any candy. I wasn't expecting trick or treaters."

"Aw, that's okay. I just wanted to show you my costume anyways."

"How about if I make it up to you with ice cream from Potter's?"

"Cool!"

"C.J.?" Jill's voice was strained. "Why don't you run down to the marina and show Brew your costume before he goes home?"

"Okay." He lifted his hand in a wave. "Bye, Dr. Adam."

"Bye. Have fun tonight."

"Don't stay long, C.J. And meet me at the car."

"Okay." The boy was already at the bottom of the stairs.

Light from inside spilled over the tension in Jill's face. "Don't make promises to him, Adam. Don't make a date with him."

"Why not?"

"Because he believes. He'll count on it."

"There's no reason he shouldn't." Adam had a feeling they weren't talking about C.J. or ice cream now. "What's really on your mind?" Sex was on his. It shouldn't be, but no one was perfect.

"About the other night," she said, folding her arms over her chest. "It can't happen again."

"I see."

"No, you don't. There are reasons. A lot of them."

"It's not necessary to justify anything to me. If the spark isn't there…"

"This has nothing to do with sparks. It's a distraction and I can't afford that right now."

"Right now? What's changed?" Adam wasn't sure why he felt the urge to push back. She was right and he had his own reasons for putting on the brakes.

"The thing is…" She caught the corner of her lip between her teeth. "Before… With the other doctor… I let myself have feelings. It had been a long time since I put myself out there. Everything was fun and flirty, but all of a sudden there was a future to think about and it made me happy. Then, he said he was leaving. Small-town life wasn't for him."

"He was an idiot. Probably still is."

"I agree. But my little boy thought the sun rose and set on that idiot and he just walked away."

Adam had thought he was past having to reassure her that he wasn't leaving. "We've been through this."

"That was before we— You know." Now she was shy and awkward as opposed to uncomfortable.

"You're right. The 'you know' does change things." He knew exactly what she was saying. "And I agree that it can't happen again."

"You do?"

He nodded. "You're a single mother. I think I know you well enough to know that an intimate relationship needs to mean something. You just talked about a future. And there wouldn't be one with me."

She looked surprised, but said, "Okay."

She'd felt the need to explain and so did he. "I'm divorced. College sweetheart."

"Why didn't it work out?"

"I have a complicated relationship with my parents. That

sounds so stupid, but we're all a product of our environment." He sighed. "In any other family, my academic accomplishments would have been considered stellar, but not with my folks."

"I know how brilliant and accomplished your family is." She'd done the background check.

"I put a lot of energy into not caring about their approval. I told myself that the effort I was putting into being at the top of my class was only for me, that I didn't care what they thought about my life and my choices. But my parents loved Judith Bennett. Even my grandmother was a fan. So I proposed and we were happy right up until I didn't meet her expectations."

"So she turned to someone else? There was another man?"

"I think that would have been easier to take. I chose a medical specialty that she didn't consider special." He remembered the betrayal on Judy's face when he broke the news that he wanted to be a family practice doctor. "She thought she was marrying into a family of high achievers and that I would be famous like the rest of the Stones. Obviously we had a failure to communicate. Failure leaves a mark when you're a Stone, so now I make sure to put all my cards on the table. No assumptions, no misunderstandings."

"What are you saying?"

"Marriage isn't something I'm interested in doing again."

"Good to know." Her voice was steady, but there was a bruised look in her eyes and he hated himself for putting it there.

"It's for the best."

"I agree straightforward communication is the way to go. For me that's about C.J."

"What about him?"

"He's my first priority. His welfare and happiness."

"So you've said."

"But it's more important now." She blew out a long breath. "After you left the other night, I realized how easily C.J. could have found you there. He'd have asked questions."

"Kids aren't easily fooled."

"I dodged a bullet this time, but taking another chance isn't something I'm willing to do. If we continue seeing each other, he'll get ideas about you, me, a future. Believe me, he doesn't need encouragement for that, but there's no win in this situation, especially since you've been completely honest about your intentions. I don't want him hurt."

Adam understood and respected her for protecting her child. "He's a great kid. I like hanging out with him."

"For now. But what happens when you don't?"

He knew she was referring to the other doctor who'd hurt them both. "That's not going to happen. I moved here because of the small-town life."

"And you spent summers here, so you knew what you were getting into." She settled her purse more securely on her shoulder. "But no one knows better than me that there are lots of ways to leave even if you're still here."

"Mom?" The small voice carried up the stairway. "It's time to go trick or treatin'."

"Coming, sweetie." She smiled, but the look was brittle around the edges. "Thanks for understanding. Bye, Adam."

He watched her stiff back as she descended the stairs. Shouldn't he be more relieved after the straightforward talk? Now she knew he was a confirmed bachelor and he was completely on the same page with her about not setting C.J. up for a fall. Everybody was happy.

He should be, but not so much.

That warm and gooey feeling inside could turn on you in a heartbeat, Jill decided.

She should be pleased that Adam had been so understanding about ending any future physical relationship. Maybe she would be if he hadn't dropped his own bombshell.

Married? Really? And no one knew this? She'd done the background, but the marital status came up single, not divorced. And why did it really matter? At least she found out he wasn't on the market before her heart got sucked in and she got hurt. Maybe a little hurt. Nothing that spending time at this Halloween party couldn't fix, although if she'd known it would be necessary to hide her hurt feelings from people who knew her too well, she'd have planned to wear a full face mask.

Children and adults were gathered in the town hall, which was located one street over from Main, next to the courthouse. Hanging from the ceiling were orange-and-black streamers, cobwebs and tissue paper ghosts. One fourth of the big room was partitioned off into a haunted house, complete with zombie guide, squeaky door and eerie laughter sound effects.

On tables along the wall, potluck food was set up. On the other side of the room, games for the younger children were in progress. C.J. was with a group of boys in the corner who had dumped already-inspected candy from their trick-or-treat pumpkins. Tyler was there and it looked as though the two of them were in negotiations for a major trade.

Jill was checking out the choices on the food table, although her appetite had been missing since that informative chat with Adam. The mayor stopped beside her, paper plate in hand.

"Hey, Jill. How are you?"

"Good," she lied. "Yourself?"

"Can't complain. Technically, I could, but who would listen?"

"I would," Jill volunteered. She'd rather focus on someone else's problems than her own.

"I'm really fine." The sad gray eyes said something else.

It was said that eyes were a window to the soul, and with a flash of insight, Jill somehow knew that Loretta Goodson had loved deeply once and it hadn't ended well. She wondered if her own experience with Adam Stone had somehow made her more perceptive. It certainly made her empathize.

"What's going on with you? I haven't seen you since the football fundraiser at Potter's Ice Cream Parlor, before Maggie's baby was born. Have you seen her yet?" the mayor asked.

"Yes, but just for a couple of minutes. I remember how it feels when you're so tired you can't see straight and want to cry with the newborn, but you're the grown-up and can't."

Her Honor looked wistful. "I've heard it's really hard."

With the new insight Jill realized she'd touched a nerve with the mayor and a change of subject would be good. "The baby is beautiful and healthy. Or so Adam says and he's the expert."

"How is that hunky health care professional who's renting your upstairs apartment?"

"Still renting it." *For now,* Jill added to herself. When she'd left him earlier, he'd seemed far too relieved that she was ending it before anything really got started. And she didn't want to talk about Adam. Getting him out of her head would be better. *Good luck with that,* she thought bitterly. "What's new, Your Honor?"

"Still trying to get that golf course and club idea off the ground, but so far I can't get anyone to commit resources to the project."

"That would create some jobs, which would be a good thing." Jill felt the sluggish economy just as much as every business owner in town.

"More leisure activities would boost tourism, but it would also attract the retired demographic, which is good for construction. More folks moving here would pump money into the town's existing infrastructure." The mayor sighed. "It's giving me gray hair."

"Oh, please. Don't even complain about yours." Jill tugged on a lock of her red hair sticking out from under her hat. "Compared to mine, yours should be in a national ad campaign for product."

"Thank you." Loretta grinned. "And for this flattering shade of brown I'm incredibly grateful to Susie at A Wild Hair. On a man, gray hair is distinguished. A silver-haired woman isn't a fox, just old. It's my plan to keep everyone guessing about my age, but not out loud or to my face."

Jill laughed. "C.J. thinks anyone over twelve is ancient."

"Ah, the world according to a six-year-old. To be that innocent again."

Jill wasn't sure she'd ever been so innocent at that young an age. She remembered hearing her mother cry on those nights her father didn't come home and the fights on the nights he did. Finally he just left and her mother looked sad. As a single mom, she knew it was important that she not bring any pain or distress into her son's life. He might not get the male influence or the family he craved, but there was something to be said for a stable environment.

"So C.J. had the stitches removed from his chin all right?" The mayor took the tongs from a bucket of chicken and put a drumstick on her plate.

"He did," Jill confirmed. "And the jury's still out on who was more traumatized, him or me."

Loretta glanced at C.J., roughhousing in the corner with his friend. "It's purely an observation, but I'd say Dr. Stone worked magic on that boy since he's dressed for Halloween as a health care professional."

"I have to admit Adam was really good with him. And you can hardly see the scar on his chin."

"And what about your scars?" Those sharp gray eyes didn't miss much.

"I'm doing fine." If you didn't count sleeping with Adam, loving every minute of it and telling him not ever again.

"Has Adam worked his magic on you?"

Jill shook her head. "I didn't split open my chin."

"No, your wounds are on the inside where no one can see them."

There was no arguing with that, so she didn't try. "I'm fine."

"But are you happy?" Loretta's voice was kind. "Dr. Stone is an attractive man. I know there are people in this town who haven't welcomed him as warmly as they might have if you hadn't been hurt by that one who shall remain nameless. There's no reason to believe that this one will abruptly pick up and leave."

"Are you trying to talk me into going after him?" Jill stared at the older woman. "Since when does your job description include matchmaking?"

"It's a chick thing, not a mayor thing." Loretta grinned. "In my humble opinion you and Adam Stone would make a lovely couple."

"And if it didn't work out, what happens to C.J.?"

"You can't protect him from everything, Jill, and if you try it's not doing him any favors."

"Keeping my son from harm is in my job description."

"Absolutely—to a point. But you can't surround him with bubble wrap. Sure, you take a chance and he could get hurt and mope around. It might even leave a scar on the inside like the one on his chin. But it's experiences that give him the character to deal with what life will throw at him. He needs to learn that not every kid on a team with a losing record should get a trophy. That's not a realistic view of the world."

"Every child needs to know he has value."

"I couldn't agree more. But they need to find goals and work for them. You can't give C.J. his self-esteem, he's got to earn that on his own. Like you. Taking over your mother's business, raising your child and taking classes for your degree. I can't tell you how much I admire what you're doing. And what an amazing example you are to your son."

Jill knew the words made a lot of sense and she appreciated the approval. "Thank you, Your Honor."

"And while I'm on my soapbox, let me give you some words of advice. No one can guarantee that Dr. Stone will be any different from the doctor who disappointed your little guy. But he's here now and we might as well use him."

She was pretty sure Her Honor, the mayor, wasn't talking about sex, but the fact that Jill's thoughts went there wasn't comforting. How did she protect herself from that?

Chapter Ten

Adam was driving too fast and his tires squealed when he turned off Lakeview Road and into his driveway. Jill's car was there and he parked beside it. He was frustrated and pissed off. On top of that, it was late and he was tired. There was a gnawing in his gut that was mostly about feeling powerless and a little about being hungry.

He turned off the car then got out and slammed the door harder than necessary. Walking around the corner, he saw the lights on in Jill's place. That didn't help the gnawing in his gut.

Every night Adam walked up the steps to the porch that led straight to her front door and bypassed it for the stairs up to his place. The difference tonight was that it was harder than normal to head for the stairs and not stop to knock on that door.

Behind it Jill and C.J. ate dinner, laughed and talked. It should be the little guy's bedtime, but maybe he got to stay up a little later on Friday night since there was no school the next day. Now Adam knew what it was like to hang out with them.

He knew what it was like to make love to her.

Temptation pulsed through him, but he tamped it down and took the stairs two at a time. He unlocked his door and flipped the light switch on the wall just inside. There was a small table where he usually dropped his mail, but he couldn't do that because he had forgotten to stop and get it.

"Damn it."

Turning lights on, he went to the kitchen, opened the fridge and grabbed a beer. After twisting off the cap, he took a long pull of the cold brew. It did nothing to smooth out the edges of his aggravation or the emptiness in his belly.

He yanked open the freezer hoping a complete microwavable meal in a box would be there. Since he hadn't been to the market, it would take a loaves-and-fishes miracle to accomplish that. The best he could do was a couple slices of ham on stale wheat bread. He slapped a sandwich together and ate it standing up. Not nearly the gourmet quality of hot dogs and mashed potatoes, but it took care of the hunger if not the gnawing emptiness.

He needed to do email and, beer in hand, headed to his second bedroom that was used as an office. On the way he heard a knock on the door. A couple of thoughts flashed through his mind. If there was a medical emergency, someone would call.

It was too late for C.J. to be there and Jill wouldn't let him come upstairs, per their agreement about not giving him ideas. She wouldn't be there, also per their agreement. He opened the door and saw Jill standing there with a big box in her hands.

Adam had never been happier to be wrong. "Hi."

"This wouldn't fit in your mailbox, so the postman left it with me. Mail, too." She nodded at the envelopes on top.

"I'd have come down to get this." He took the box from her and set everything on the table beside the door.

"No problem. I thought something that heavy might be important."

"Books." He liked to read, but lately that was more about filling up the long evenings than pleasurable leisure time.

"Okay. Well, I heard you come home and just wanted you to have your mail. Landlady duty fulfilled."

"Right. Thanks. You should get back to C.J."

"Actually, Ty asked him to sleep over since tomorrow is Saturday."

"Ah." Adam nodded. "So Cabot has the boys."

"He took them to the high school football game," she explained. "The kids love that. They get to run around like wild Indians and fit right in with the Blackwater Lake High mascot, which conveniently happens to be an Indian. Cabot gets to watch the game and relive his glory days as star quarterback."

"Yeah." He hoped the boys had been running around and were not aware of what had happened on the field at the beginning of the game.

"What's wrong, Adam?"

"Just a bad day." He finished the last of his beer, then held on to the bottle and stared at the label.

Jill was half turned away from him, leaning toward the stairway, poised for a quick escape. Her body language all but screamed that she really didn't want to be here. There was reluctance in her voice when she asked, "Do you want to talk about it?"

"Wouldn't do any good."

"You're sure?" She took a step back.

"It's just frustration. Comes with the territory." But when

that territory could be different, it was damned hard to let go of the restlessness and discontent. "I'm okay."

"You don't look okay."

"Really?"

"Yeah, really," she said. "Your mouth is all pinchy and tight. There's a look in your eyes like you want to put your fist through a wall."

"Interesting diagnosis, Dr. Beck. I thought medical school taught me how to assume an indecipherable poker face."

"Not so much. Either you need a poker face refresher course or whatever happened that made your day really bad got to you more than it normally would."

"Probably all of the above." He blew out a long breath.

"Now you're scaring me." She studied him carefully. "Did you lose a patient?"

"No," he said quickly.

She was shaking and the cold air made white clouds of her breath. "Then why the bad day?"

"Something happened at the football game."

"Oh, no—" Shivering cut off her words.

"Come inside before you freeze." He curled his fingers around her upper arm and tugged her forward.

"O-okay."

He shut the door and said, "I'd offer you wine or hot tea, but they're only on my grocery list and not actually on premises yet. Beer?"

"No, thanks."

"Then the best I can do is a seat on the couch in front of a fireplace without a fire." If he'd known, he'd have made one.

"I'll take it." She moved farther into the room and looked around. This was the first time she'd been inside since showing him around. "Love what you've done with the place."

"Really? It's just furniture. I haven't had time to deco-

rate—" He saw the teasing in her eyes. "Oh. That was sarcasm."

"Just a little." She sat at the far end of his brown leather
sofa. "Tell me what happened at the game."

"I'm surprised you haven't heard. It's all over the local
news." He sat down, too, but left as much space as possible
between them. Feeling the warmth of her skin would likely
bring on temptation that would jeopardize their fragile understanding. "One of the football players, Jimmy Kowalski,
broke an ankle. Or I should say a linebacker on the oppos-
ing team did it for him."

"Oh, no." Her expressive face filled with sympathy.
"Aren't there emergency medical technicians on hand at the
games?"

"Yeah. They stabilized him on the field and then provided
transport to the closest medical facility. I got the call and met
them at the clinic."

"I don't mean to be insensitive, but physical contact is
part of the game. And the single most important reason C.J.
will never play it. But I don't understand why this got to you
so much."

"The X-rays showed that both bones in the leg are broken
and will require surgery to repair." Feeling helpless made him
angry all over again. "He's a senior and hoping for a football
scholarship because his father is out of work and without one
he can't go to college. All I could do to help was ship him off
to the hospital, which is close to a hundred miles away. So,
on top of the trauma and pain, he gets plenty of time on that
drive to worry about a surgery and its effect on his future."

"I can understand a little of what his parents feel." She
slid over and narrowed the space between them on the sofa.
"When C.J. cut his chin we would have had to make that
drive if you hadn't been here."

"That was different."

"Why?"

"Because I could help C.J. A family practice doctor is sort of a jack-of-all-trades, but orthopedics isn't my specialty. All I could do was confirm that it was worse than a simple break, immobilize the leg and give him something for pain."

"I'd say you fixed the immediate problem. He can't thrash around, possibly doing more damage. And he won't be hurting on the way to the hospital."

"I hated shipping that kid off." He curled his fingers into a fist. "The situation really sucks. In a big city everything necessary would be under one roof."

"You could still be in the big city if you wanted. Or go back," she said.

"I just get angry when I feel helpless. That's not what I want." He saw traces of the wariness she'd worn like a cloak since the first time he'd seen her. Part of her was still protecting herself and probably always would. "The best-case scenario would be for that kid to be here in Blackwater Lake among family and friends."

"You really do know this community, don't you?" She smiled as if he were the star pupil.

"I'm getting there." He shook his head. "And what else I know is that this town is into skiing, snowboarding, boating and water sports—activities which aren't particularly userfriendly to bones. If Blackwater Lake is going to attract development, the scope of medical services has to expand. I know that small-town sensibilities and big-city services are in conflict with the growing pains. And that high school kid is caught in the middle. It makes me mad but there's no one to be mad at and that's even more frustrating."

"Ginny always says don't get mad, get even."

"Virginia is quite the philosopher," he said diplomatically. "What does that even mean?"

"I think in this case it's about channeling energy into finding a way to change circumstances that you don't like."

"I knew that." He shrugged. "On some level where I wasn't too angry to think straight. But in this case change will take time, but mostly money."

"So how do you get it?"

"Mercy Medical Center Corporation needs to approve a position for an orthopedic specialist for the clinic. And Blackwater Lake needs to step up and make the bureaucrats see that. It's an investment in the future. *I* need to get involved and make that happen."

"See?" She smiled and put her hand on his arm. "No more frowny face. You look better already."

"And you look beautiful as always." Did he really just say that out loud?

The way her eyes widened said he did. While they stared at each other, the warmth of her fingers penetrated the material of his long-sleeved shirt. It felt too good and he didn't just mean her touch. Having someone to talk to was a rare comfort, an extraordinary pleasure. He'd been lonely, but that was nothing new for him and wasn't really a factor in how he felt about her.

And he didn't want to lose the privilege of having her in his life. "It's getting late, Jill."

"Yeah." But she didn't move.

"If you don't go now, I'm going to kiss you. I made a promise not to do that and I need your help to keep it."

"Right." She blinked twice, then stood and hurried to the door. "Good night."

No, not good, he thought. Now the scent of her was in his house as well as his head. That was going to make it even harder to resist her than it already was.

Early Saturday morning Jill left C.J. at the marina with Brewster to visit Maggie Potter and her baby girl. And now she was sitting in the state-of-the-art glider chair with the infant in her arms.

"I love her name. Danielle Maureen. I bet your mom is excited."

"She's been so anxious to be a grandmother and Brady isn't cooperating."

"That's because he isn't married and not showing any signs that he wants to be." Jill snuggled the little pink bundle to her chest and breathed in the indescribably sweet scent of her skin. "I don't think there's anything more wonderful than holding a tiny, warm baby in your arms or that special smell babies have."

"Oh, she's made some extraordinarily special smells," Maggie said, grinning.

"You're already a high achiever, Dani Mo." The little girl continued to stare up at her while valiantly trying to suck on a tiny fist. "She is just more beautiful than I can even tell you."

"Really?" Her friend sat on the chocolate-brown sofa nearby.

Jill met her gaze. "We're friends, Maggie. I wouldn't lie about something like that."

A new mother's anxiety had replaced the sadness in her brown eyes. "Even if she was so homely she'd have to wear a bag over her head to go to preschool?"

"Oh, please." Jill stroked the baby, snugly swaddled in a pink receiving blanket. "She's already gorgeous. On a baby beauty scale of one to ten, she's easily a twenty-five. How could she miss with parents like you and Danny?"

And Jill could have smacked herself because the sadness was back in her friend's eyes.

"I wish he could have seen her," Maggie said.

"Oh, sweetie, I'm sorry. I didn't mean to remind you or make you sad about something so happy and wonderful."

"You don't have to remind me. The memories surround me

every day." She looked at the pine logs that formed the walls of her home. "When Danny built this place, he took extra care with the bedrooms for the two kids we were planning to have, making sure to double insulate so they wouldn't get cold."

Maggie's house was a log cabin a couple of miles from town, and Danny had done all the work himself. The floors were pine and had brightly colored oval braided rugs throughout. A crocheted afghan in multiple shades of green was thrown across the back of the sofa where Maggie sat. In the stone fireplace, flames crackled and popped, giving the room a cheerful warmth that didn't reach her eyes.

Jill effortlessly moved the glider chair forward and backward. She looked into the baby's big serene eyes that were so much like her mother's, at least for now. "I believe wherever he is, Danny can see his daughter. He's her guardian angel."

"I know, right?" Maggie scooted forward on the couch. "He sent Adam Stone here to work at the clinic because there would be a snowstorm and I couldn't get to the hospital."

Jill wasn't sure Danny had sent the doctor, but he was definitely here. And he had been there for her friend. "Everything went okay with the birth, he said."

"Normal in every way," Maggie confirmed. "But Adam was so calm, so steady, that he kept me calm and steady. I know it was a textbook delivery and probably Ginny could have handled it, but I'd never had a baby before. Having a doctor there gave me peace of mind. I'm so glad you were wrong about him leaving town at the first sign of winter."

"I was more wrong than you know." If he'd left, she wouldn't have slept with him and wouldn't now be so badly wanting more. "But I wasn't the only one who misjudged him. The whole town felt the same way."

"Not everyone," her friend reminded her. "I gave him the benefit of the doubt and not just because he's a good customer. You have to admit that Mayor Goodson never had a bad word to say about him."

"Is this an election year?" Jill asked wryly.

"Never alienate a potential voter. Political rule number one. But it's more than that."

"I know. But I don't trust him." Jill thought about Adam and what he'd done. In the spirit of fairness, she shared. "He shoveled snow off my walkway after being up all night delivering this little girl."

Maggie's gasp was teasing. "Clearly he has underhanded intentions."

"And that's not all."

"Tell me more."

"He prescribed some kind of medication for Hildie Smith that apparently gave her an attitude adjustment. Brew has a twinkle in his eyes and a spring in his step. He pretty much thinks Adam walks on water."

"Oh." Maggie covered her mouth with her hand, faking shock. "Skullduggery afoot."

"No kidding." Jill rolled her eyes. "Just last night I went upstairs to bring him his mail—"

"Do you go to his apartment often?" Maggie's eyes sparkled with innuendo.

"First time since I showed him around. Anyway, I could tell he was upset about something and finally got him to talk."

"Did it involve flashing him with a little skin?"

"It didn't." *Not that time anyway,* Jill thought. "He took it pretty hard that one of the high school football players was hurt in the game. Adam couldn't really help because orthopedics isn't his specialty and the kid had to go to the hospital so far away."

"Yeah, it's not exactly convenient when you're giving birth in a snowstorm either," Maggie said wryly.

"Turns out Adam is going to work on a plan to expand

the clinic and eventually build a hospital right here in Black-water Lake."

"Sounds like a man ready to run out on us at the first op-portunity," Maggie teased. "Watch out for that one."

"Okay, I'll admit my judgment about him is flawed." Jill thought for a second. "The thing is, he seems very sincere about his long-term plans here in Montana."

"You think?"

"I'm afraid to consider anything where Adam is con-cerned. I've been fooled before and I can't afford to slip up with him again—"

"Again? You're not talking about the last doctor." Maggie studied her friend. "You slept with Adam Stone, didn't you?"

"No."

"You're so lying."

"How do you do that?" Jill just shook her head in awe. She hadn't said anything incriminating, yet her friend had busted her big-time.

"I know you. Tone of voice. Guilty body language. Pen-sive frown that means a questionable decision, probably in regard to behavior." Maggie shrugged. "Was it when you played mail lady and the doctor upstairs?"

"No," Jill said. "It was when the doctor shoveled snow for his landlady."

"And how was it?"

"I'm sure it was a lot of work and his back was sore after he finished."

"No. I meant the sex and you know it."

"Oh. Sex. Actually it was pretty amazing." The earth moved, Jill remembered. And she saw fireworks. "But he and I agreed that it can't happen again."

"What?" Maggie's voice rose and brought a whimper from the baby, who was starting to show signs of discontent. "Sorry, Dani, but seriously. Auntie Jill needs to have her head examined."

"You know how I feel. C.J. and I are doing fine. Why let someone in and chance rocking the boat?"

"I don't say this lightly because I'm a mother now, too. I completely understand this maternal love that makes you want to surround your child with bumper guards and keep him safe." Maggie met her gaze. "But you can't protect him from everything and everyone forever."

"That's what Loretta Goodson said." Maggie raised the baby to her shoulder when she started to fuss. "She said when life throws him a curve, he won't have developed the skills to deal with it."

"Wow." Maggie's expression was filled with awe. "I wonder how she acquired so much kid wisdom without kids of her own."

"I'll ask her sometime."

"Take notes," her friend advised. "Now, back to the doctor. I think everyone realizes that he's not going anywhere. You don't need to hold back your feelings—or anything else."

"You're wrong, Mags. The reason he agreed we can't—get personal—again is that he's a confirmed bachelor. Carrying on with someone and settling for less than a committed relationship isn't the message I want my son to get."

"It's a valid concern. Again, motherhood does give you a different perspective." Maggie nodded thoughtfully. "But I just need to say a couple of things before I stop ragging on you."

"Okay, shoot." Jill steeled herself for the lecture.

"First, don't borrow trouble."

"If I do, does that mean I have to give it back?"

"Smart aleck." She shook her head. "It means you've already written an ending to the story. But you can't see the future any more than anyone else can. You have to take the journey, take a chance."

Jill wondered if Maggie would do it all again if she'd known what she knew now about how hard it was to lose the man you loved. But that wasn't a question she could bring up.

Instead she asked, "What's number two?"

The sadness returned to Maggie's eyes, clearly indicating that this part had to do with the love she'd lost. "This is one thing I know with my whole heart and soul. If you don't live in each and every moment, you're not really living at all. Don't miss an opportunity. Don't let yourself have regrets."

In spite of the fact that Maggie's wisdom had come from tragic personal experience, she wasn't recommending surrender.

When Dani started a full-on wail, Jill handed her over so her friend could breast-feed her baby. She missed having the warm body in her arms. She'd never been anyone's wife, but loved being a mother, and it made her sad that C.J. wouldn't have a brother or sister. She was sure of that because, in spite of her friend's sad insight, Jill had a different take on it.

She couldn't, just couldn't, throw caution to the wind and risk being hurt, no matter how much she might want Adam to hold her and kiss her again.

Chapter Eleven

Adam stepped off the last stair onto the porch just in time to see Jill coming around the corner of the house hefting an eight-foot ladder.

"Stop right there," he ordered, then hurried over. "Why didn't you ask for help with that?"

She brushed a strand of red hair off her forehead and huffed out a breath. "First of all, I do this all the time and don't need help. Second, I wouldn't bother a tenant with something like this. It's Saturday."

"What's your point? The ladder is still heavy and I'm stronger than you."

"My point is that I wouldn't disturb you on your day off. Maybe if there was a fire or the threat of a meteor strike. Possibly a NASA satellite hurtling toward the house. Otherwise, no."

He grinned at her. She was possibly the only woman on

the planet who could make him smile when she was telling him to mind his own business.

"First of all," he said, echoing her words, "I'm pretty sure that we're also friends in spite of the fact that I give you money every month and you let me live under your roof. Second, if you hurt yourself carrying something that's too heavy for you, I won't be off because I'll get called in to work. On you." He walked closer and put both hands on the ladder, stopping short of taking it away. "Where do you want this?"

"You're awfully bossy."

"It's one of my best qualities." The stubborn look in his eyes said he wasn't letting go.

"In the house." She stepped away and smiled. "Thanks, Adam. It is heavy."

"Don't mention it. I'll follow you."

Partly so he'd know exactly where to put it, but mostly to check her out from the back. The Blackwater Lake Marina sweatshirt she had on was pretty shapeless, but those jeans were perfect. If looking at her butt was an Olympic sport, he'd get all tens because practicing would be easy. He could watch all day. The only thing better would be cupping those soft curves in his hands, and his palms tingled now from wanting so badly to do it again.

"You okay?" she asked when he tripped on the top porch step.

"Fine." Distracted and disgusted with himself maybe, but all in one piece.

Watching where he was going was important and he didn't just mean right this moment. He had to keep focused. Eyes on the prize, which was building credibility along with a career in Blackwater Lake. No detour with his lovely, sexy landlady because it could cost him the fragile and hard-won respect of the people in this town.

Inside the house, she walked down the hall and stopped

beneath an access panel in the ceiling. "If you could set it down right here, that would be great."

The front door opened and slammed shut, followed by the sound of six-year-old feet running through the living room.

C.J. came to a screeching halt in the hall. "Dr. Adam!"

"Hey, champ. What's up?"

"I was at the marina with Brew while Mommy went to visit Maggie and baby Dani. Then I saw you carryin' the ladder for her. Whatcha doin'?"

"What are we doing?" he asked her.

"Furnace filters. They need attention twice a year, before summer and winter," she said. "I'm actually late this year. That snowstorm threw me off schedule, but fortunately it's all melted now and I'm good to go. Saturday is chores day and I've got a long list."

"Okay." Adam put one foot on the bottom rung of the ladder. "I'll get it down."

"Wait. I thought you were just carrying the ladder for me."

"Now I'm volunteering for chores duty."

"You don't have to do that," she protested.

"I know." He climbed until he could reach the metal closures for the vent. When he slid them sideways and it dropped, he saw the metal filter. "This isn't the disposable kind."

"In my humble opinion these are better quality. I hose them off. Just lift it out and hand it down."

"I wanna help," C.J. said.

"Hold on, champ." Adam did as Jill instructed, but handed the lightweight square filter to the boy and said, "Take that out back by the hose. There's another one in the living room, right?"

"How did you know?"

"I wish I could say I'm psychic, but upstairs is the same

floor plan. In fact, we might as well do those, too." He braced himself for another protest.

"You're sure you don't mind?"

There was nothing on his day-off agenda except possibly a movie all by himself. "I'm sure."

He moved the ladder and took out the filter behind the living room vent, then handed it to C.J., who was quivering with excitement while he waited. The boy took it outside and returned just in time to see Adam at the front with the folded ladder.

"Where ya goin'?"

"Don't bother Dr. Adam, kiddo." Jill put her hand on the boy's shoulder, a subtle cue to stay put.

"The filters in my apartment need cleaning, too," Adam explained.

"I can help, just like I helped now."

Adam knew the job would go faster if he did it by himself, but the eagerness and vulnerability in that small face tugged at him. With his chin tilted up, the scar was visible and Adam suspected there were more on the inside that didn't show. His mom, too. The kid was soaking up the attention, craving the male bonding just as Jill had said. The chore might go faster alone, but alone wasn't all it was cracked up to be.

"Okay, C.J.," he said, "Let's go upstairs."

"What can I do?" The boy followed him out the door.

"Same thing you did in your house. It saves a lot of time if you're there. I don't have to climb down the ladder. You're a really big help."

"That's 'cuz I'm six. Pretty soon I'll be seven. Mommy said in a couple of weeks."

"What do you want for your birthday?"

"A video-game player for the TV," he said without hesitation.

Adam knew it was pricey. "Have you told your mom?"

"Yup." The boy reached up and took the square filter.

"Just set that by the door. We'll get the other one and take them both down for hosing off. I'll leave the ladder here to put them back up after they dry."

"Okay."

"What did your mom say about the player?" he asked, folding the ladder to move it to his living room.

"Nothin'." C.J. shrugged, but he wasn't any better at hiding his feelings than his mom. "She asked what else I wanted, but that just means I won't get what I really want."

Adam could easily afford it and almost said so. He stopped just in time as an idea occurred to him. "Maybe you could do some extra chores for me and earn the money to buy it."

"Really?" The hope in those bright brown eyes could steal a heart if you weren't careful.

"Maybe."

"What do you want me to do?"

"Give me a chance to talk to your mom. If she's okay with it I'll come up with a list."

"Oh, boy!"

This time Adam followed C.J. downstairs and carried the filters. It was one thing to take a handoff, another to hang on and navigate stairs when you were six going on seven. They took them out back, where Jill was just putting the first two in the sun to dry.

"Hey, you," she said to her son.

"Mommy, Dr. Adam is going to give me stuff to do so I can make money."

"What?"

"For my game player," he clarified.

Adam liked it a lot better when she smiled. There wasn't a hint of a smile now and he felt the need to explain. "I can help and figured it would give him a sense of accomplishment."

"I see." The tone of her voice said she wasn't happy about

whatever it was she saw. "C.J., it's time for your favorite chore of the whole week."

"Aw, Mom. Do I hafta clean my room?"

"Yes. Now scoot."

Apparently he knew resistance was futile because he said, "O-okay." Then he looked at Adam. "I won't be long."

When they were alone, Jill's eyes filled with something, but it wasn't the anger he'd come to expect. If he had to name the emotion, he'd say dread. Apprehension.

"What's wrong?" He took a step closer.

"You know the game player he wants is expensive and that I can't afford it."

"From what he said, I connected the dots."

She lifted a hand to her forehead to shield her eyes from the sun that was dropping lower in the sky. "Don't think I don't appreciate the gesture, but taking care of what C.J. wants is my responsibility."

"I'm just trying to help," he defended.

"Not a good idea." She shook her head. "I'm the one he depends on."

The only one he can depend on. She didn't say that, but he read between the lines. "Jill, I—"

"Please don't." She held up a hand to stop the words. "This subject isn't up for debate. Thanks for helping with everything today. Now I better go supervise. To a six-year-old, cleaning his room means playing with the toys scattered around. Short attention span."

When she walked inside, Adam was less interested in her butt than her story. It was the first time that had happened. No matter how much reassurance and evidence to the contrary, she just wouldn't let go of the idea that he was leaving. He was no shrink, but it didn't take one to know that she'd been deeply hurt by someone who walked out on her, someone other than "the last doctor." He intended to find out just what had happened to her, mostly because he was curious and wanted to help if possible. But part of his motivation was just being selfish.

Adam badly wanted to sleep with her again, but he'd given his word that he wouldn't. If only words would make the temptation go away. He had a feeling Jill was fighting the attraction, too. An agreement made with all the good intentions in the world wouldn't hold up to a double dose of desire. When sex happened again, and it would happen, she was going to have to be the one to break the bargain.

Jill wasn't quite sure how they ended up at Blackwater Lake Hardware late in the afternoon. Chores were completed and before Adam put away the ladder he asked about changing batteries in the smoke detectors, pointing out that it should be done twice a year. Some people thought when the clocks were turned ahead and back was a good rule of thumb, but for her it could be filter cleaning. She agreed.

Since she didn't have the required 9-volt replacements, the doctor offered to drive her into town. If C.J. hadn't overheard, she could have gracefully declined, but... Oh, who was she kidding? Adam offered and she didn't want to decline, gracefully or any other way. So she was going to hell.

They walked past a winter preparedness display and Adam was carrying the two-handled blue basket. "What about flashlights and extra batteries? Snowstorms can snap tree limbs and bring down power lines."

"I know," she said. "And as far out as we are, you can be stuck for a few days. Sometimes it takes that long for the plows to get to us. If you don't already have snow tires now might be a good time to get some. Phone reception can be spotty, too, cell and landlines."

He picked up a flashlight. "So that's a yes?"

"The old one broke." When she nodded, he set it beside the package of square batteries in the basket.

"Can I have one, Mommy?" C.J. looked up at her with pleading in his eyes. "It's dark outside and I really need to see where I'm going so I don't fall and hit my chin and need stitches again."

"Wow, that argument was well thought out and emotionally motivated," Adam said, his voice full of admiration. "I see a career in law someday."

"When he's a lawyer, he can buy all the flashlights and batteries his little heart desires, but until then..." Jill sighed. "For now I have to say no. You can use mine, kiddo."

Looking into two pairs of eyes—one brown and disappointed, the other blue and wanting to offer help—Jill felt as if she was letting everyone down. Adam had just been trying to help earlier. The idea of giving C.J. chores to earn the money for something he wanted was a good one and showed great father instincts for a guy who had no intention of being a father.

Maybe that's why she'd gotten so defensive, that and her independent streak. Counting on anyone else was setting herself up for a big fall. She hated denying her son anything, but her budget was pretty tight and she still had to squeeze out enough for his birthday presents.

She added flashlight batteries to the basket. "I think that's all we need. Let's go pay."

Moving ahead, she got to the front of the store first. The kid behind the cash register was a stranger to her, but apparently he knew Adam.

"Hi, Doc."

"Hey, Landin. How's it going?"

"Could be better. Jimmy's out for the rest of the season."

"I know. Got a call from the orthopedic specialist at the

hospital." Adam didn't say more, probably because of patient privacy issues.

Obviously he was talking about the football player with broken bones. This kid was a tall, skinny, brown-haired teen with gray eyes and a cute smile who didn't look big enough for football.

"There goes our division championship. He's the best wide receiver we've got."

"Wait and see. Maybe John McLaughlin can step up. He's in good shape and pretty fast." How did Adam know all this? The question must have shown on her face because he said to her, "I did the team physicals before they started practicing. How could I not go to the games?"

That explained it. Apparently the teens embraced him in a way the adults loyal to her hadn't. When the kid gave her a total for the purchases, Jill swiped her debit card, then keyed in the PIN. Before she could take her bag with receipt, Adam grabbed it.

"Good luck next week," he said.

Landin nodded. "We'll need it."

A cold wind hit her when she walked out the front door toward Adam's SUV at the curb. Then C.J. hit her with something else. "Mommy, my tummy's so hungry."

"We're going straight home now and I'll make dinner," she promised.

"I can't wait. It's too far." In his uniquely dramatic way, her son dragged his feet and limped along as if about to drop from lack of nourishment.

Jill met Adam's amused gaze. "He goes from zero to starvation without any warning."

"Growing boys will do that." He snapped his fingers. "I've got an idea."

C.J. stood up straight. "Is it ice cream at Potter's?"

"Close. How about dinner at the Grizzly Bear Diner?" Adam met her gaze. "My treat. It's the least I can do."

"And why is that?" she asked wryly. "If anything I owe you for helping out with chores today."

"Give me a minute. I'll think of a reason."

"How about you just like takin' us to the diner?" C.J. suggested.

"That works for me." Adam grinned at the boy.

It worked for Jill, too. Way better than she wanted. For the second time that day she didn't have the will to decline. "Thank you, Adam. That's really nice of you. But, C.J., it's a block down Main Street. Do you really think you can walk that far being so hungry?"

"Yeah!" He took off at a run.

"Stop at the light," she called after him.

"'Kay, Mom!"

Side by side, she and Adam walked at a brisk pace mostly because it was cold. Jill wanted to snuggle into him for warmth and kept fighting the urge. It seemed so natural; he made everything seem so natural. She was getting awfully tired of fighting.

C.J. was already waiting for them up ahead at the red light on Pine Street. "Hurry up, you guys."

"Your son is pretty fast," Adam commented. "I wonder if he can catch a ball."

"He's not ever playing football. I'm pretty sure a parent has to sign a permission slip or something if a student is under eighteen."

"Good luck with telling him no." Adam's hand brushed hers and when he slid his fingers into the pocket of his jacket, it crossed her mind that he felt the temptation, too. "He struck out on the flashlight tonight, but give him time. He'll have a few years to perfect his pitch and I wouldn't want to be in your shoes if he decides to play."

They finally reached the corner and when the light turned green the three of them crossed the street to where Grizzly Bear Diner took up the corner. Inside it was warm and very crowded.

"Apparently this is the happening place," she said.

Even if one didn't know the diner's name, a theme would be obvious. There were bears everywhere. Wallpaper, menus and logo T-shirts on the employees.

Jill knew the hostess behind the podium displaying the sign Please Wait to be Seated. "Hi, Mrs. Taylor."

"Hey, Jill." The older woman gave the man behind her a wide smile. "Hi, Dr. Stone."

"Hi, Iris."

Iris?

"It's nice to see you." Iris Taylor was under five feet tall and in her late fifties.

"Same here." Adam met her gaze. "How are you?"

"Doing great. Now," she added. "That prescription you gave me really helped the pain from my arthritis."

"Good." He looked around the crowded waiting room. "Are there always this many people?"

"It's Saturday. I guess you're here for dinner." There was a curious expression in her eyes when she made the connection that Jill and C.J. were with him. "Three of you?"

"How long is the wait?"

"I'm really hungry, Mrs. Taylor," C.J. said.

"I bet you are. About thirty minutes." She looked at her list with some of the names highlighted in hot pink. "But for you, Doc, I think I can find a booth pretty quick."

"Thanks." He looked down at the boy, who was peeking into the glass case displaying grizzly bear T-shirts, sweatshirts and figurines. "Starvation can set in pretty quick when you're six."

"Give me a minute. Can you hang on?" she asked C.J.

"I could if I had one of those bears to play with," he said to his mother.

Jill rolled her eyes and knew by the sparkle in his that Adam was thinking, *Watch out when the kid wants to play football.*

Five minutes later Iris led them out of the waiting area and past the counter with swivel chairs. Carl Hayes, the plumber hired by her mother to do the upstairs work when Adam's apartment was being built, sat there.

"Hi, Mr. Hayes," she said.

"Howdy, Jill." The balding man smiled and lifted a hand in greeting. "Hey, Doc. Carl Hayes," he said.

"I remember," Adam said. "How are the leg cramps?"

The older man swiveled his counter stool around to look at them. "It was the darnedest thing. Vitamins, Gatorade and water sure did the trick just like you said. I've been sleeping like a baby ever since I saw you."

"Excellent news." Adam grinned. "Keep it up."

"Don't worry. I couldn't stop even if I wanted to. My wife keeps shoving water and vitamins at me."

"Good for her." Adam laughed and shook his hand.

They made it a little farther toward the back before a gray-haired man called out, "Hey, Dr. Stone."

Adam stopped at the end of a booth. "Mr. Gerard."

"Call me Alan. This is my wife, Winnie."

"Nice to meet you," he said. "How are you feeling, Alan?"

"Stomach pain is gone. More fiber is just what the doctor ordered." He laughed at his joke.

"That's good to hear. It's important. Nice to meet you, Winnie."

"Same here. I've got an appointment at the clinic next week," she said. "Nothing serious. Just my yearly checkup."

"I'll look forward to seeing you."

"Jill's a nice girl. And that little guy of hers is a hoot," the woman told him.

"I know." Adam waved a goodbye, then turned to her.

Jill felt the warmth in her cheeks. Could the matchmaking be any more obvious? She wished the earth would open and swallow her whole. Agreeing to come here was a mistake on many levels, but mostly she tried not to resent the fact that these people were *her* friends, supposedly loyal to her. But they were treating "the new doctor" like a rock star. She followed Iris to a booth in the back and slid into it. That's when she realized Adam and C.J. weren't behind her.

He'd been stopped yet again and was chatting with someone she didn't know. His hand was on C.J.'s shoulder in a friendly, familiar way that tugged at her heart. The little boy had lifted his chin, pointing to the place where Adam had stitched it up, and people were admiring a job well done.

Adam looked comfortable, as if he'd known everyone for years instead of just months. He fit right in and she hadn't done much to help except being seen with him here in the diner that one time. He had gained town confidence all on his own.

She was happy for him. Really. It was just that now her already complex feelings grew even more complicated. The last doctor she'd dated hadn't stayed past the first snow, which made him a wimp and an outsider as far as this town was concerned. When another single, good-looking doctor showed up, everyone circled the wagons around her and she felt safe, protected. Now Adam was no longer an outsider. Blackwater Lake embraced him as one of their own and he had their loyalty. Like her. It was a level playing field.

And she'd seen tonight that her friends and neighbors were putting them together as a couple, a family, which made the potential for pain shoot way up. When things with Adam didn't work out, and she refused to let herself believe that they could, she would let down the whole town.

Just like when C.J.'s father had walked out.

Chapter Twelve

All the way home from the diner C.J. kept up a nonstop monologue and Jill wasn't exactly sure when he took a breath, but the words kept on coming.

"When can we go to the hardware store again?"

"Next time we need hardware. Aren't you tired?" she asked.

"No."

"My ears are tired."

"You're funny, Mom. How can ears get tired? Are yours tired, too, Dr. Adam?"

"I think my ears are more used to it because I listen to patients all day." He was the soul of diplomacy.

"My ears aren't sleepy at all," C.J. said. "And next time we go to the hardware store, I hope we can go to the Grizzly Bear Diner, too. It was fun."

"And now it's late," Jill said. "I need to get those batteries in the smoke detectors."

"I'll do it." Adam turned the SUV into the drive, then came to a stop beside her car and turned off the ignition.

"Can I help?" C.J. piped up from the backseat.

"It's time for bed." Jill wanted desperately to be by herself, distance herself from Adam.

"But, Mom, it's too early to go to sleep."

"Don't forget about your shower." She released her seat belt and opened the front passenger door.

"But Dr. Adam needs me to help him put the new batteries in. Right, Dr. Adam?" C.J. opened the right rear door and jumped out.

"I'm Switzerland." The interior light illuminated Adam's wry expression as he met her gaze.

"Huh?" C.J. looked up for an explanation.

Jill couldn't help smiling. "That means he's not taking sides, kiddo."

"But, Mom, I hafta watch. How else am I gonna learn?"

Why couldn't she be Switzerland, too? Jill wondered. And why couldn't it be a country without guilt? A place where a mother could give her son a man in his life who wouldn't leave, a man he could count on. Right now she lived in the land of reality and a decision had to be made.

"Maybe just this once, since it's Saturday."

"Yay!" C.J. ran toward the front steps and called over his shoulder, "Hurry up, Dr. Adam. I don't have all night."

"Right behind you, champ." Adam laughed as he fell into step beside her. "If only I had that much energy."

"Yeah."

And if only Adam's arm didn't brush hers. The touch made her yearn for the right to snuggle closer to his lean strength. But that was part of a relationship, and all she had with Adam was sex, followed by a verbal agreement not to let it happen again.

While Adam took her son upstairs to replace his smoke

detector batteries and bring down the ladder, Jill unlocked her front door and went inside. She turned on lights and set her purse and the bag with the new flashlight on her desk. The quiet surrounded her and that wasn't about C.J. not being here. It was a sign that she was getting used to Adam being around. How did one go about growing *un*accustomed to a charming man who wasn't hard on the eyes and had a great sense of humor?

Ten minutes later the front door burst open and C.J. came in. "Mom? We're here and Dr. Adam brought the ladder."

And made it look incredibly easy because he *was* stronger than her. "I can see that."

"He let me climb up it."

"Not by himself," Adam assured her.

"Dr. Adam had to do the battery 'cuz I can't reach it yet. But I watched really good."

"It would have been a lot harder without his help. I needed the extra weight to steady the ladder so I could connect the battery."

C.J.'s freckled face beamed with pleasure. "Let's do the rest!"

Jill watched her son race out of the room, and his enthusiasm nearly broke her heart. It was all about having a man to do guy stuff with. In the kitchen, C.J. climbed the ladder and Adam was right there to make sure he didn't fall. Each time they went through the process, she marveled at his protectiveness and patience considering the chore took five times longer because a little boy wanted to help.

If there was a way to resist this doctor, she'd give almost anything to know the secret because falling in love wasn't something she ever wanted to do again.

"Okay, C.J., your reprieve is over. Now you really do have to get ready for bed."

"But, Mom—"

"No buts." She pointed in the direction of his room. "March. Or there won't be time for a story."

"Can Dr. Adam read it to me?"

"That's your call," the doctor in question said.

"You've already done too much."

"I was happy to help out."

She shook her head. "We've monopolized your day off."

"I didn't feel monopolized. It was fun hanging with you guys."

"And we appreciate everything you did, but you probably want some time to yourself."

"Solitary isn't all it's cracked up to be."

It sounded an awful lot like he was saying he'd really wanted to be there, but that was the very hardest thing for her to believe.

"C'mon, Mom. Just tell him it's okay."

She looked at her son and the heartbreaking hope so visible in his eyes. How could you say no to that? "Okay."

"Awesome." Without another word he turned and ran toward his bedroom. Several moments later she heard the sound of the shower.

"I'll put the ladder away," Adam offered.

"Thanks."

"Don't mention it."

C.J. was finished showering when Adam came back. With wet hair slicked down, teeth freshly brushed and wearing Superman pajamas, he looked up at the tall man. "I'm ready for my story now."

"Good, because I'm ready to read."

They all trooped down the hall with the redheaded child in the lead. Jill folded the bedspread down and pulled back the covers while he chose a book from his shelf.

"I want the baby animal book," he told Adam before climbing into bed.

"Looks like a good one." Adam waited until he was all tucked in before sitting beside him.

Jill stood nearby, listening to the sound of his deep voice as he read the child's story. She fell further under his spell with every word. When he read "The End," she wasn't ready for it to be over any more than C.J. was.

"Dr. Adam?"

"Yeah, champ?"

"Where do babies come from?" A question clearly designed to stall just a little longer and who could blame him? Certainly not Jill.

Adam looked at her. "Have you discussed this?"

"A little," she said.

"Mommy told me that the man has a seed and the woman has the egg and when they love each other a baby happens." C.J. yawned.

Adam looked relieved. "Your mom is exactly right. I have nothing to add."

C.J. yawned again before saying, "Dr. Adam, did you have a dog when you were six, almost seven?"

"Yes."

"I knew I was old enough for a puppy."

"I didn't say that." Adam pulled the covers more snugly over the small chest. "I had an older brother and a sister to help with the responsibility."

"Dr. Adam, is it—"

"Enough," Jill interrupted. "Lights out, kiddo."

"O-okay." He rolled onto his side.

"Good night, C.J." Adam gently brushed the hair off the child's forehead, then stood and backed away from the bed.

"I love you." Jill moved forward and kissed her son's cheek. "Sweet dreams. See you in the morning."

"Love you, Mommy." His eyes drifted closed and he said sleepily, "See you tomorrow, Dr. Adam."

Please don't count so much on tomorrow, she wanted to tell him. Just because Adam was doing all the right things to put down roots in Blackwater Lake didn't mean he would be part of their lives. She'd gone down that path and been fooled before.

She followed Adam out of the room and pulled the door nearly closed. Then she led the way into the living room to see Adam out.

"Free at last." She tried to make her voice light and breezy but didn't quite pull it off.

"What's wrong, Jill?"

"How do you know anything is?"

"Your mouth is tight. Your tone is tense. And your forehead has frown lines." He gently touched his fingertip to a spot just above her eyebrow.

If he hadn't done that, saying good-night would have been almost easy, but he had to go and lay a finger on her.

"You're way too observant. I thought I was hiding it pretty well." Resentment tinged her words as she met his gaze and the stubborn set of his jaw. "You're the toast of Blackwater Lake. At the Grizzly Bear tonight it was clear that you've bonded with the people of this town. You're everyone's new best friend."

"And you were hoping I wouldn't be?"

"It's not that. Not exactly."

"Then what?" He nudged her chin up when she tried to look away. "You haven't done a great job of hiding the fact that you're holding back, refusing to get attached. Tell me why. And before you start, I know it's not about the last doctor."

"You're right." She slid her fingertips into the pockets of her jeans and sighed. The words came with surprising ease. "My father left my mother and me when I was about C.J.'s age."

"So you were abandoned."

"I had my mom. And friends here. But, like so many other people, I have abandonment issues." It was a weak attempt at humor, but she couldn't manage a smile and didn't want his pity.

"Not having a father leaves a hole in a kid's life." He wasn't asking a question.

"Yeah." She nodded. "It hurt. And more than anything I wanted my child to have a traditional family. There was a time when I thought it would happen, too."

"But it didn't."

"Right in one." Her heart hurt for C.J. "I fell in love with Buddy Henderson when we were juniors in high school and thought we'd be together forever. Everyone in town expected us to get married the spring after graduation. Then the spring after that."

"Why didn't you?"

"He never proposed. But Blackwater Lake expected a wedding. Especially after I got pregnant."

"He still didn't ask you to marry him?" His blue eyes darkened with anger.

"It's hard to propose when you're not around."

"He left?" Surprise mixed with fury in his voice.

"When I needed him most," she confirmed.

"Son of a bitch—"

"My sentiments exactly." She met his gaze and willed him to understand. "C.J. never knew his father but I remember mine. I know what it's like to blame yourself when someone you love, someone you believe with all your heart cares about you, walks away. That's why I don't want *him* to get attached."

"I see." Adam rubbed a hand across the back of his neck, then nodded. "Thanks for telling me."

"Thanks for listening."

She would never have believed that explaining everything would lift a weight from her heart, but it actually did. Maybe confession was good for the soul.

"For the last time," he said, "I'm not leaving."

She smiled. "Okay."

He put his hand on the doorknob and the intensity in his eyes said loud and clear that he would stay if she asked. "If there's anything else you want to talk about—"

There was something she wanted, but it had nothing to do with talking. She remembered what Maggie had said about living in the moment so life wouldn't pass her by. Adam was simply too tempting to resist.

Jill moved close and put her hand on his chest, then stood on tiptoe and touched her mouth to his. Simmering desire exploded into flame and he wrapped his arms around her, then kissed her as if he'd been starving for this and could devour her. She felt the same way. Breathing hard, she broke off the kiss and took his hand in hers, leading him toward her bedroom.

Adam stopped and looked down at her, his eyes intense. "Are you sure about this? We talked about 'you know.'"

"I remember." She smiled because all the rational arguments in the world didn't seem to matter in this moment. "We both said it couldn't happen again."

"We both have our reasons." He reached out and tucked a strand of hair behind her ear. "Are they still a problem for you?"

"No." She was tired of fighting what she felt. Tomorrow regrets might come, but tonight she wanted him. And sometimes wasn't it okay to be selfish? "Is it a problem for you?"

"No."

She gave him a flirty look and said, "Then quit stalling, Doctor."

Without another word he tugged her into the bedroom

and locked the door behind them. In what had to be a world record they undressed each other and crawled into her bed, under the quilt. The sheets were cold against her back, but Adam was there to warm her.

He brushed his hand up and down the bare skin of her side, barely touching her breast. She moaned, a sound of need that couldn't be held back. It was like pouring gas on a fire, making the flames burn higher and hotter. His hands were everywhere and he never stopped kissing her. When he slid inside, she was ready, wanting and willing. She lifted her hips and wrapped her legs around his waist, drawing him in deeper.

They moved together in a frantic, sensual rhythm that pushed her to the edge, where she gladly stepped off. His breathing was a rough rasp in her ear and she gloried in the sound and feel of his hard chest pressed to her soft curves. In what felt like a heartbeat she came apart as pleasure exploded through her body. Seconds later Adam followed her over and they held on to each other through the aftershocks, too spent to move.

Finally he lifted his weight to his forearms and grinned down at her. "That was pretty good."

"Is that your expert diagnosis, Doctor?"

"You think I'm an expert?"

"Oh, yeah."

"Okay, then."

He went into the bathroom and she missed his warmth in the bed. Moments later he was back and pulled her against him. She settled her cheek on his chest, content and sleepy and happy.

The next morning Adam woke up with Jill curled against him. It was a little past six-thirty and the house was quiet. Obviously C.J. was still asleep, just like his mom, he thought. Her red hair was a mass of curls against the pink flowered pillowcase and he ached to run his fingers through it again because he wanted her again. But he kept his hands to himself and let her sleep. Anyone who worked as hard as she did needed the rest.

He needed to get out of here before her son woke up and started asking questions more complicated than where babies come from. Still, he couldn't resist just a few more seconds of watching while her guard was down. She looked so young and innocent, too young and too innocent to be the mother of an almost seven-year-old and carrying a whole lot of emotional baggage from getting dumped on and abandoned.

Adam had taken an oath to do no harm, but five minutes alone and no questions asked with the jerk who'd left her alone and pregnant was really tempting. How could any guy do that, especially to Jill? It wasn't just looking so vulnerable while she slept that made him want to protect her. He felt the same way when she was wide-awake and arguing with him until hell wouldn't have it.

He knew his decision to relocate to Blackwater Lake was a good one. He loved it here and wasn't pulling up stakes, but she'd pointed out that there were lots of ways to leave that had nothing to do with geography. He didn't know where things were going with Jill, didn't know if he had it in him to commit to someone again and risk another mistake. It seemed unfair to pursue anything and chance hurting her when his track record was less than stellar.

Glancing at the clock on her side of the bed nudged him into action since the digital display was inching toward seven o'clock.

"Gotta get out of here," he whispered to himself.

He eased out of bed and dressed quickly, leaving his shirt untucked. His cell phone was still clipped to his belt because he'd been in such a hurry to have her. With shoes in hand, he unlocked the bedroom door and tiptoed out. It bothered him to leave without saying goodbye, but a note? What would he say? Thanks for last night? See you later? Nothing seemed right.

He put his shoes by the front door and went to the kitchen. The least he could do was get the coffee ready to go for her. That was a statement, although what it said or why he was making it were less clear. Something to do with being happy and wanting to do a nice thing for her. How sappy was that?

After filling the water reservoir in the coffeemaker, he measured grounds into a filter and closed the lid.

"Good morning."

His heart stuttered at the sleepy, sexy female voice, but that was nothing compared to what he felt when he turned around. Her hair was tousled in that way a woman's hair should be the morning after making love the night before. Her eyes had the heavy-lidded, well-pleasured look of a satisfied female and made him want to satisfy her again.

"I was trying not to wake you," he said when finally able to form words.

"You didn't." She smiled and her expression was more contented than he'd ever seen. "I actually overslept. I'm usually up earlier than this."

"Good. I'm glad." That came out wrong. He was usually more articulate than this. "I mean that I'm glad I didn't disturb you."

She sure disturbed him—sound asleep or wide-awake. Right this minute he was disturbed because she was wearing a robe and he really wanted to know if she was naked underneath. The fuzzy, peach-colored, floor-length thing had a zipper up the front and it would be so easy to...

"Why don't you turn on the coffeemaker and stay for a cup?" she suggested.

He knew it wasn't the best idea, but was too grateful for the invitation to say no. "Don't mind if I do."

Almost instantly after he flipped the switch, the machine started to sizzle and drip. Jill moved beside him and opened the cupboard above to pull down two mugs. The scent of her filled his head just like last night when he'd held her and loved her. It wasn't just sex, but for the life of him he couldn't define what "it" was.

She set cream and sugar, spoons and napkins on the table. "Are you hungry?"

Loaded question, and he hoped the knot of need inside him didn't show on his face. "Maybe."

Color crept into her cheeks and the pulse in her neck fluttered, telling him she knew exactly what he was thinking. When the coffee was ready, she picked up the pot, her hand unsteady as she poured the rich, steaming liquid into the mugs. Then they sat down at the table and stared at each other without saying a word.

She picked up her mug and blew on the steaming coffee before taking a sip. "It's good."

"A skill acquired out of necessity during my medical training."

"When your wife left." It wasn't a question.

"Yeah. Right around then."

"Did you miss her?"

"I didn't have time to think about her." That wasn't really an answer but it was partly true.

He thought about it now, his wife walking out because the specialty he wanted so badly wasn't flashy, prestigious or high profile enough for her. He remembered coming home to an empty apartment and realized that he hadn't missed her or been especially hurt. Moving on with his life had been easy, which made him merely stupid for choosing her in the first place. The problem was that he hated feeling stupid.

"Mom?" C.J. stood in the kitchen doorway rubbing his eyes. When he stopped and looked, his face lit up and all traces of sleepiness disappeared. "Dr. Adam! Are you havin' coffee?"

"Yes." Adam was grateful that the question was simple and he merely had to confirm the obvious.

"Did you come over for breakfast?"

That one was harder to answer truthfully since he'd actually never left.

Fortunately Jill bailed him out, but her brown eyes sparkled with the mischief of their secret. "I'm going to make scrambled eggs, bacon, hash browns and toast for Dr. Adam."

"Awesome." That seemed to be the kid's new favorite word.

"I'll be right back." As she walked out of the room, Jill said over her shoulder, "Just talk amongst yourselves."

C.J. climbed up on the chair. "I'm glad you're here."

"How come, champ?"

"'Cuz I like eggs and Mommy doesn't make them very much."

"Why?" Adam figured it was a time issue.

"I don't know." The boy shrugged his small shoulders. "But I guess this is a special occasion."

Definitely special, Adam thought, and not just for the food. "I'm looking forward to it. Your mom's a good cook."

C.J. nodded slowly. "I got a really good idea."

"What?" Adam sipped his coffee.

"You should come to my birthday party. Mommy's makin' lasagna. Brew and Hildie are comin'. And Maggie." He wrinkled his freckled nose. "She's bringin' the baby, though."

Adam struggled not to smile at that. "Is the baby a problem?"

"Boy, is she!" The kid sighed dramatically. "Tyler said she cries all the time. And poops. It's pretty stinky."

Apparently Cabot and Maggie were friends if they'd gone

to visit the new mom and baby. "I can deal with noisy and smelly."

"Really?" C.J.'s eyes widened. "You mean you'll come to my party?"

"I wouldn't miss it for anything."

"Awesome!"

"Thanks for inviting me."

C.J. was giving him a rundown on what he wanted for his birthday when Jill walked back into the kitchen wearing jeans and a sweater. He missed the sensual mystery of what was or was not underneath the robe, but the way she filled out the denim was a pretty good trade-off.

She got to work cooking while he and C.J. set the table. The smell of frying bacon filled the kitchen, and his stomach growled, telling him he was hungry for food, too. And something else that was less basic and easy to identify. Something more elusive. He just knew that hanging out with Jill and her son filled him up in places he hadn't known were empty.

His phone rang and he hoped it wasn't a patient emergency, which was never good, but he was looking forward to a home-cooked breakfast that wasn't oatmeal or toast. He pulled the phone from the case and looked at the caller ID, but the number was blocked.

After pushing the talk button and putting the phone to his ear, he said, "Dr. Stone."

"Hello, Adam. This is your grandmother."

He hadn't heard from Eugenia Stone since his move. "Is everything okay?"

"No. But if that was an inquiry about my health you'll be relieved to know that I've never been better."

"I'm glad to hear that." Adam shrugged when Jill gave him a quizzical look. "So what's up?"

There was static on the other end of the line for several seconds, but he caught the last words. "…arriving around noon. Pick me up at the Blackwater Lake Lodge at one-thirty."

She was on her way?

He had questions, so many questions, and started to ask, but the line cut out again, then dropped the call. Soon enough he'd find out why she was coming, although he had a pretty good idea.

Jill turned a piece of bacon sizzling in the pan, then looked at him. "Is there a problem?"

"That's a very good question."

"Who was on the phone?"

"My grandmother." He ran his fingers through his hair. "She's on her way to Blackwater Lake."

Chapter Thirteen

Jill knew the sound of Adam's car. When she heard it pull into the drive, she waited for footsteps on the porch, then discreetly peeked out the front window. It was hard to see all the details she wanted while trying not to be seen herself, but she managed to form a general impression of Adam's grandmother. Eugenia Stone was a tall, trim woman, probably in her seventies, and wearing a navy crepe pantsuit and matching low-heeled pumps. They moved out of sight and up the stairs to Adam's place, so the woman must be in pretty good physical shape.

"Show's over," she said to herself. "Time to get back to work."

She sat down at the computer to finish the statistics assignment due the following day. Unfortunately focus for the tedious task was hard to come by. She'd spent the most wonderful night of her life in Adam's arms. That morning she'd awakened with the place beside her in bed still warm from his body and the spicy scent of his skin filling her head. He'd made her coffee, for goodness' sake, and seemed eager to stay for breakfast. God help her, she'd actually allowed the thought into her head that it was what being a family would feel like.

Then his grandmother showed up. He'd mentioned once that his family wasn't pleased he'd moved to Blackwater Lake. They'd probably sent an emissary to bring him home.

C.J. ran into the room and for once she was glad he'd interrupted her train of thought. "What's up, kiddo?"

"I'm bored. Can I go down to the marina and see Brew? Please, Mom?"

"Sorry. He's doing inventory and can't keep an eye on you today. How about watching TV or reading a book?"

"Do I hafta?" The expression on his face said he'd rather go to Mercy Medical Clinic for more stitches in his chin.

"No. But I have computer work to do, so you're going to have to entertain yourself for a while. Quietly."

"I can't be quiet." He flopped on the couch with a dramatic sigh.

"We've talked about this, C.J. I have to—" A knock on the door interrupted the lecture she hated having to deliver again. She stood and walked over to answer it, saying over her shoulder, "That's probably Brew. Maybe he's finished with inventory and can hang out."

"Awesome."

But when she opened the door Brewster Smith wasn't on the other side. "Adam—"

"Hi." He reached out and ruffled C.J.'s hair. "I want you to meet my grandmother. Eugenia Stone, this is my landlady Jill Beck—"

"And I'm C.J."

"Ms. Beck." The older woman had silver hair and blue

eyes the same shade as Adam's. She took Jill's measure, then looked down. "What do those initials stand for, young man?"

"What are nishuls?"

"His name is Christopher John, but everyone calls him C.J.," Jill explained. "It's a pleasure to meet you, Mrs. Stone."

"Thank you. May we come in?"

"Of course. I'm sorry. Please." She stepped back and opened the door wider. Adam walked in behind his grandmother and sent her a sympathetic glance.

The older woman looked around the room, and the sharp gaze no doubt missed nothing. "My grandson told me a lot about you."

"Did he? I'm sure it was all good." If you didn't count the very beginning. Jill noticed the corners of his mouth curve up. At least one of them was amused.

C.J.'s expression was filled with rampant curiosity. "I don't remember my grandma. I only saw pictures 'cuz I was a baby when she died."

"That's too bad, young man. Grandmother and grandson is a very special relationship."

Adam put his arm around the older woman's shoulders. "I'm her favorite grandchild. Right, Grandmother?"

"I love all my grandchildren equally." But her grave expression softened when she looked at Adam. "You were and always shall be a rascal."

"Are you movin' to Blackwater Lake?" C.J. asked her.

"Goodness no."

"Then why are you here?" the child wanted to know, not the least bit intimidated.

Jill couldn't say the same. She considered herself a strong woman who could deal with raising a child by herself, running a business alone and not backing down from anyone. But Eugenia Stone scared the living daylights out of her and that could only mean one thing. This woman's good opinion mattered, and that wouldn't be the case if Jill didn't have feelings for Adam.

"May I sit down?"

Jill gave herself a mental forehead slap. "Yes. Please. Can I get you anything? Coffee? Tea?"

The older woman sat on the couch. "Nothing, thank you."

One by one C.J. looked at the adults in the room. "Are you guys just gonna sit around and talk?"

"That's how people become acquainted, young man. I would like to get to know your mother."

"Then I have an idea," he said. "How about if Dr. Adam and I go outside and play ball? That way I won't interrupt when you're talkin'."

"Oh, sweetie—" Jill put her hand on his small shoulder. "Dr. Adam wants to visit with his grandmother because he doesn't get to see her as much as he'd like."

"On the contrary," she said. "We have time to catch up. I think that's a wonderful idea, Christopher. Why don't you take the child outside, Adam?"

"Really?" He gave her a skeptical look. "You don't mind?"

"Not at all." She looked at Jill. "We'll have a chance for girl talk."

"Yuk." C.J. raced out of the room and came back moments later with his mitt. He handed the ball to Adam. "Let's go."

"Have fun, you two," the older woman said.

"Be good, Gram," he said playfully on his way outside.

"I always am." Her voice oozed cool confidence.

The door closed and Jill wished with all her heart that she could go with them. "Are you sure I can't get you anything, Mrs. Stone?"

"Thank you, no. Please sit. I'd like to chat." She looked at the expanse of sofa beside her.

Jill sat and tried to think of something to say that wasn't about herself. Clearly the Stone family of Dallas had money and manners that would set too high a bar for a girl from Blackwater Lake, Montana, who had a child outside of marriage.

"Your son is very cute."

"Thank you."

"He reminds me of Adam when he was that age." There was a wistful expression on the woman's face. "Not in looks, but that mischievous personality."

"He's a handful," Jill said fondly. There were several moments of awkward silence before she thought of something to fill it. "How was your trip?"

"Grueling. This isn't an easy place to get to, is it?"

"I suppose not." Jill felt the judgment vibes big-time, and the need to defend her home became uncontrollable. "Some people find the peace and quiet of a small town appealing. We often get visitors who come here for a break from big-city stress."

"There's something to be said for a hospital and an airport nearby," the other woman pointed out.

"It's not perfect, but no place is."

"The Dallas Metroplex comes very close."

Jill could read between the lines and couldn't help pushing back. "Obviously you're very happy living there, but Adam wasn't."

"In my opinion, he simply needed to get the back-to-nature phase out of his system. He'll come to his senses."

"That's what I thought originally. In fact I told him the first hint of winter would have him throwing in the towel and heading for the hills, but I was wrong." Jill remembered that time in the beginning, using her hostility against his charm. Now her antagonism was gone, leaving her with nothing to power her anti-Adam shield. "Not only did he stay, but he delivered my best friend's baby in a blizzard, then came home and shoveled snow off my walkway."

"I know that dewy-eyed look, Ms. Beck. And I feel it's my duty to warn you it would be unwise to start picking out wedding invitations and china patterns."

Jill badly wanted to tell this woman what she could do with her warning. Fury vibrated through her until she was shaking with it, but no way would she show weakness. She linked her fingers to stop her hands from trembling, then settled them in her lap.

When under control, she met the other woman's gaze and refused to look away, keeping her tone cool when she asked, "What makes you think I want to marry Adam?"

"Because he's quite a catch. Handsome. Rich. A doctor."

"Apparently he wasn't enough for his ex-wife."

"So, he told you about that." His grandmother's mouth pulled tight, deepening the lines around her mouth. "Stupid girl."

Jill was surprised to find any common ground with this woman, but she totally agreed with that. "Her loss is Blackwater Lake's gain."

"Not for long. His family is not happy about this decision."

"That's unfortunate because Adam seems very happy with it."

"Maybe temporarily. It's my impression that he's—oh, what's the word? Infatuated with you, Ms. Beck. But that won't be enough to keep him here. He will come to his senses and return to Dallas. I assure you of that."

"You're wrong, Mrs. Stone. He's worked very hard to make himself a part of this community. People here don't trust easily, but when you finally earn it, it's yours forever. Adam has earned it. The man I know and—" Love? She couldn't go there. Not yet and maybe never, but she had to say what was in her heart. "He's content right where he is."

"You're wrong, Ms. Beck. And sleeping with him isn't

love." She stood and gracefully walked toward the door. "I truly hope you don't get hurt when he realizes his mistake."

The only reason Eugenia Stone got the last word was that Jill was stunned into silence because the other woman knew she and Adam had sex. When she was done being stunned, Jill's insecurity kicked in, fueled by the old woman's words. Letting herself think about a family with Adam was like writing a prescription for heartbreak. She should have known better.

Based on her experience, she should have known that when things were going well it was time to run in the other direction.

While driving his grandmother into town, Adam pointed out the scenic beauty of Blackwater Lake and the towering, snow-tinged mountains beyond. Her only comment was, "Hmm."

Maybe she was speechless with awe, but he didn't think so. This place filled up his soul, but the difference in people was what made being a family practice doctor interesting and challenging. It was possible that Eugenia Stone's soul was stirred by looking at the ocean. Or flowers. Or a closet full of designer shoes. Or maybe she didn't have a soul.

That wasn't fair. She'd been good to him; he was her favorite. And he loved her very much.

She was sitting at rigid attention when he glanced over to the passenger seat. It was on the tip of his tongue to ask why she was here, what the purpose of the visit was, but she'd only say that she didn't need a reason to come and see her grandson. After that she'd add something snarky about it being difficult to visit a destination in the middle of nowhere.

"So, how's the family?" he asked instead.

"Fine. Mostly."

This part of the road leading into town was winding and

he had to keep his eye on it, so looking at her expression to read between the lines wasn't an option. Questions were required.

"Mostly fine? Or mostly not fine?"

"Your mother is well. She's in the process of losing ten pounds for your brother's wedding."

"So Spencer has set a date?"

"It seems Avery has her heart set on being a June bride."

"I wish someone had let me know," he said.

"Consider yourself informed now."

When his brother and Avery O'Neill had visited Dallas, his grandmother had been traveling and didn't meet her with the rest of the family. Since Spencer was clearly head over heels in love, Adam assumed Eugenia had corrected the oversight. "What do you think of Avery?"

"Charming girl." There was real warmth in her tone. "Smart as a whip. Witty. Pretty. She's absolutely perfect for Spencer."

And how did she feel about Jill? Adam only wondered because there'd been tension between the two women. After he and C.J. came back inside, it had been impossible not to notice the coolness.

He wasn't going there. Why open that can of worms since he had no intention of declaring any intentions? "Okay, so Mom and Spencer are fine. That leaves Dad and my twin, Becky. Which one of them isn't fine?"

"Both."

"What? Really?" This time he did glance at her because the road was straight and just entering the town of Blackwater Lake. Her mouth was pulled tight, which he didn't much like.

"Your sister and her husband are going to marriage counseling. No one will tell me why they need it."

And Adam wouldn't either. His sister had confided in them about her husband's one-night stand, but she didn't want their grandmother to know. Becky was confident the marriage could be saved and Eugenia Stone held a grudge if anyone had the audacity to wrong a member of her family. And she took her grudges very seriously. She'd treated his ex-wife like her own daughter, but when the marriage ended, some very unladylike language had come out of his grandmother's mouth. No one could speak his ex's name in her presence.

Adam only said, "I think Becky and Dan will be able to work things out. They have demanding careers and twins of their own. Taking time for them as a couple isn't easy, but it's necessary to the relationship."

"Speaking of relationships… Can we talk about your land-lady?"

"Look," he said. "There's the Blackwater Lake Lodge."

"Don't get me started on the things wrong with that place."

"Okay. Tell me about Dad." Maybe he'd successfully deflected the personal question.

She sighed loudly. "Other than the fact that he won't listen to me or your mother?"

"About?"

"He's working too hard and won't slow down. He's tired all the time and won't see his doctor for a physical. So far our nagging has been unsuccessful."

"It sounds like you and my mother need to nag harder."

"It won't work. I'm his mother. I know."

"Has Spencer talked to him?" If he tuned out his wife and mother, maybe he'd take the advice of one of the country's leading cardiothoracic surgeons.

"I think your mother is coordinating that endeavor."

"I'll talk to Dad, too. We're both doctors."

His grandmother waved her hand dismissively. "You and your brother may be physicians, but you're also his children and by virtue of your youth, you don't have the life experience to give him perspective."

He could see where this was headed and decided to change the subject again. Potter's Ice Cream Parlor was just coming up on the right and there was a convenient parking space out front. He pulled into the diagonal lines. "How about some ice cream?"

"I'd love some. If it's good," she added skeptically.

He'd inherited his love of the stuff from her and knew her high standards would be met. "Best I've ever tasted."

After exiting the driver's side, he walked around and opened the door for his grandmother. A cold wind was blowing from the north and he knew real winter was bearing down on them. Quickly he hustled her inside where it was warm, and crowded. He was surprised he'd been able to park out front.

Carl Hayes was sitting with his wife at a table for two just inside the door. "Hey, Doc, how are you?"

"You stole my line." Adam grinned. "I'm doing great. Got family in town. This is my grandmother."

"That explains the resemblance. Except I can't believe this young lady is old enough to be your grandmother." He held out his hand. "Welcome to Blackwater Lake."

She smiled warmly at the compliment. "Thank you."

"We're very lucky to have Adam here in town. He's all right."

"He is very special," she agreed.

"Nice to see you, Carl." Adam guided his grandmother to the glass ice-cream case. Maggie's brother was behind the counter, his back turned. "Hey, Brady."

The other man looked over his shoulder and grinned. "Adam. Good to see you."

"Where's Maggie?"

"In the back feeding Dani."

"Her new baby girl," Adam explained. "This is Brady O'Keefe. Brady, my grandmother."

"A pleasure." She smiled politely. "Eugenia Stone."

"Great to meet you. What'll you two have?" he asked.

She looked over the choices, then said, "A small dish of vanilla with caramel and some of that crushed HEATH Toffee Bar topping."

"The usual for me," Adam said.

"Coming right up." Brady scooped out the ice cream and set their orders on the counter by the cash register.

Adam pulled a twenty-dollar bill from his jeans pocket. "What do I owe you?"

Maggie was just walking out of the back room carrying her sleeping daughter. "It's on the house."

"I was just about to tell him that," Brady added.

"No." Adam shook his head.

"How can I charge the doctor who came through a blizzard to bring my baby into the world?" She smiled down at the little girl in her arms.

"Nice of you, but you're giving up a lot of revenue. I'm here for the long haul and one of your best customers."

"Okay." She swayed gently, rocking the baby as she thought it over. "How about a six-month cap on freebies?"

"Fair enough. And thanks." He handed over the vanilla, then picked up his own sundae. "This is my grandmother, Eugenia Stone."

"It's really nice to meet you," Maggie said. "Adam has your eyes."

"What a lovely thing to say." There was a soft expression on his grandmother's face as her gaze settled on the baby. "She's beautiful. What's her name?"

"Danielle Maureen, after my husband and my mother."

"Lovely."

"I think so. Now eat your ice cream before it melts," she teased.

"Will do." Adam grabbed some napkins from the dispenser on the counter and headed for a corner table. They sat across from each other and ate in silence for several moments.

"She's quite a beautiful young woman. Maggie," his grandmother clarified.

"She is." Adam wasn't sure if that was an observation or a comparison with Jill. "And courageous. Her husband was killed in Afghanistan before the baby was born."

"That's dreadful." Eugenia sadly shook her head. "I can't imagine how she carries on."

"Family. Her mom helps." Adam nodded toward the counter. "That's her brother picking up the slack. The people in town pitch in. Jill is her best friend and worked a regular shift when Maggie's obstetrician ordered bed rest at the end of her pregnancy. And that's on top of raising her son and running her own business by herself."

Eugenia took a bite of ice cream and chewed thoughtfully. "Speaking of that, what is the nature of your relationship with Jill?"

Mental head slap for bringing up Jill. He really didn't want to talk about her or try to define what was between them. He just wanted things to *be*. "What makes you think there is one?"

Adam had expected the question and should have had an answer ready but didn't. It would have been easy enough to say they were just friends or she was nothing more than his landlady, but he couldn't. Neither was the complete truth, but he didn't know what the truth was.

"Really, Adam, I wasn't born yesterday. Remember that life experience I mentioned?"

"What does that mean?" He hadn't been this uncomfortable since he'd been a boy trying to hide the expensive vase he'd broken.

"It means I could see the way she looked at you."

"How was that?" This was something he really wanted to know.

"Like a woman in love, or very close to it." She took a napkin and wiped her mouth. "And I saw the way you looked at her."

He didn't want to know that. Thoughts of his soul had run through his mind earlier and it was said the eyes were a window to what was inside. His grandmother probably saw that he wanted Jill. He had from the very beginning. He liked and respected her and wanted her more than any woman he'd ever met in his life. That's all it was and putting a label on it just made everything more complicated than necessary.

"Grandmother, leave it alone."

"I can't." She jammed the plastic spoon into her half-eaten ice cream. "I hate that you're here in this place without a life."

"On the contrary, I've made a life. These people are the salt of the earth. I'm proud to say they're my friends."

"You have friends in Dallas. Think about your career. You can't reach your potential here. Without a medical center and access to state-of-the-art equipment and treatment options, there's no way to make your mark and rise to the top of your field."

"If I cared about that," he countered, "I'd have chosen a more high-profile specialty. All I ever wanted was to help people. And these people need me."

"What about your needs?"

"They are what I need. There's no doubt in my mind that if I had a personal crisis they would be there for me, just like they were for Maggie Potter."

"You have family for that."

"And everyone in my family has a demanding career.

I like living in a community where neighbors look out for each other."

"Your parents and siblings love you." She folded her arms over her chest.

"And I love them. Living in Blackwater Lake doesn't change that."

"What about the Stone family legacy?" she asked quietly.

"I'm going to assume that's your way of saying that you love and miss me, too. That you wish I lived closer."

Tears filled her eyes. "Come home to Dallas, Adam. You don't belong here."

This woman had a spine of steel, or stone. He had never seen her cry, which was the only reason he didn't let his anger show. Actually, not the only reason. There was that whole wanting your family's good opinion thing.

"Grandmother, I don't want to hurt you, but not only have I found the place where I *do* belong. I finally am home."

"And Ms. Beck?"

"What about her?"

"How does she factor into your decision to bring your career to a screeching halt?"

"First of all, I haven't done that. And second—Jill is none of your business."

He was mature enough now to put the need for family approval into perspective in a way he couldn't when he was younger. That didn't mean anyone could tell him what to do. He'd make his own personal choices—as soon as he knew what they were.

Just because a woman made you feel as if you'd been struck by lightning every time she walked into the room, that didn't mean you were the man who could make her happy. Even though he was at ease and more content than he'd ever been, he didn't want to do anything to upset Jill's world. And he especially didn't want to hurt C.J. He loved that kid.

It was so much simpler with children.

Understanding women hadn't been a class offered in med school, and even if it had been available, he doubted any man could have passed the course. He only knew that since meeting Jill, it was more important than ever to get things right and not screw up.

Chapter Fourteen

Jill put out the store's Closed sign, then walked back to where C.J. was helping Brewster tally receipts for the previous month. Actually, her son had paper, something to write with and a really big imagination that kept him occupied while the older man worked.

"What's your total, son?" Brew asked him.

The little boy chewed on the pencil for a moment as he thought. "Four billion, five hundred thousand million," he said with complete conviction.

"Exactly what I got." The older man smiled down, then looked at her and simply said, "When I get all the figures and you plug 'em into that fancy spreadsheet, I'm betting you'll have black-and-white proof that profit is better than this same time last year."

"I'm glad to hear that and I hope you're right."

Improvement in business was good, but the news didn't lift her spirits as much as it once might have. Before Adam she'd have been doing cartwheels down the dock. Now? She was upset because of what his grandmother had said. It shouldn't bother her so much that the Stone family spokesperson had told her she wasn't good enough for Adam. The woman only said out loud what Jill already knew, but somehow hearing the words had been a blow to her soul.

A person could only take so many blows to the soul before it imploded.

"You okay, Jill?"

She focused her gaze on Brewster. "Hmm?"

"Looks like you're a million miles away."

"Sorry. Just thinking about something else."

"The doc's grandma?"

She could ask how he knew but in a town the size of Blackwater Lake news of Adam's grandmother arriving in a hired car was big and spread fast. Jill could deny that the unexpected visit had bothered her, but this man would just see right through the lie.

"Yeah," she finally admitted.

"That old lady didn't smile much," C.J. commented without looking up from his drawing. "Her eyes were kinda mean."

Adam's eyes, Jill remembered, but his weren't filled with disapproval. Desire maybe. Warmth and humor certainly. But did either mean anything? Eugenia Stone had warned her not to count on marriage. Marry Adam? That was jumping the gun. First, she had to be in love with him. She seriously liked him but wasn't sure what the two of them had could actually be more.

"You're awful quiet." Brewster frowned at her. "What did the woman say?"

"It was nothing."

"Meaning you don't want to talk about it." He glanced down at the redheaded child doodling on the paper.

She met his gaze and nodded. "Pretty much. Adam's family misses him" was all she said. "And I can understand that."

"Me, too. But a grown man makes his own way and everyone has to live with it."

Jill liked to think that if her son moved far away she would gracefully accept the decision and try to become part of his new life instead of alienating his friends. But... There was always a but. She wasn't walking in Eugenia Stone's shoes and didn't know what her own reaction would be.

"Well," she said, "it's none of my business."

"Maybe not." He studied her and there was understanding in his gaze. "But that doesn't stop you from thinking about it."

She would have to work this through and with all the practice she'd had that should be easy. Time to change the subject. "Thanks for staying overtime to get last month's numbers. But I've kept you too long. Hildie must be expecting you for dinner."

"Yeah."

"How is she?"

"Doin' fine thanks to your Dr. Stone."

"He's not mine," she protested.

"I'd feel a whole lot better if he was." Brewster grinned. "I think my wife has a little doctor crush going on. She's looking forward to her appointment tomorrow just a little too much."

"I'm going to tell her you said that," Jill warned.

"I'll deny it."

"But she'll believe me. Hildie only has eyes for you and it's been that way since she was fifteen."

"I know. But like she always says, old doesn't mean deaf, dumb and blind."

"Mommy, I'm hungry." C.J. put down his pencil and gave her the pathetic starving look.

"Then let's get you something to eat."

"I'm outta here." Brewster grabbed his backpack from under the counter.

Jill shut off all but one light. Then they went outside and she locked the door. "Night, Brew."

He waved and headed to his truck while Jill and C.J. walked up the path to the house. The upstairs unit was dark compared to hers with the lamp lit in the front window. A cold wind was blowing out of the north and made her shiver. Earlier Brewster had warned that a storm was coming. More often than not he was right and she didn't know how he knew. She couldn't help thinking her personal life was its own storm and she'd get dumped on soon enough.

"What are we havin' for dinner?" C.J. asked.

"I'm thinking chicken nuggets, green beans and rice."

"French fries," he said.

"We don't have any."

"Then mashed potatoes."

"They take too long to make."

"What about the dry ones?" he asked.

She knew he meant the instant kind that came in a box. "We're out of those, too."

"How come?"

"Because I haven't had time to grocery shop." Too busy hanging out doing chores with Adam on Saturday, then a visit from his grandmother today. The man had turned her routine upside down and somehow she had to find a way to make it stop.

"Do we have ice cream?"

"Yes."

"If I eat four chicken nuggets, rice and green beans, can I have dessert?"

"Yes."

"Awesome."

She breathed a sigh of relief at the successful child/parent negotiation that hadn't ended with her pulling rank. They walked into the house and she hung up their jackets on the coatrack just inside the door. She heard Adam's car coming up the drive, and her heart jolted as if defibrillator paddles had sent electricity to it.

After a couple of cleansing breaths, she walked into the kitchen and flipped on the light, then grabbed a cookie sheet from the drawer underneath the oven. Just as she reached to open the freezer she heard a knock on the door. More electric shocks and that slowed down her timing.

"I'll get it, Mommy."

"C.J., wait," she called out, but heard the sound of him running.

When Jill got there she saw Adam standing in the doorway, scooping up her son in one arm. That was because his other arm was holding a big bouquet of flowers. Her heart did another quivery little jump.

C.J. settled his small arm comfortably on that broad shoulder. "Did you bring those for Mommy?"

"Yes." He handed the cellophane-wrapped daisies, yellow-colored mums and baby's breath to her. "Beautiful flowers for a beautiful lady."

"Yuk." C.J. wiggled until Adam put him down. "Can I watch TV?"

"Until dinner's ready." Needing her distance, Jill turned and left the room.

Adam followed her into the kitchen. "What are you having?"

"Frozen chicken nuggets."

"Are you heating them up first?"

She smiled in spite of her resolve not to. Ignoring the teasing she said, "Rice and green beans round out the menu."

"Can I stay?"

"Why?" She set the flowers on the counter and finally met his gaze.

"Because I want to."

Negotiating with a grown-up man was very different from the back-and-forth with her child. "What about your grandmother?"

"I took her to dinner at the lodge restaurant and she went to her room because she's got a car coming early tomorrow to take her to the airport."

"It's very far away she pointed out." Jill met his gaze. "If you already had dinner, there's no reason for you to stay."

"Yes, there is." He brushed his finger over her cheek and tucked a stray strand of hair behind her ear.

Jill recognized desire in his eyes, and her whole body flooded with liquid heat. The vision of Adam Stone holding flowers in one arm and her child in the other had sent her straight over the edge of the cliff and into love. She hated being so damaged that her very first reaction was to pull back from something that should be joyous.

"Why do you want frozen chicken nuggets?" she asked, her voice a little breathless.

"Because," he answered, "I really want to hang out with you and C.J."

"Okay." She had to set the rules. "On one condition."

"Name it."

"Promise not to bring me flowers again."

"Are you allergic?"

Only emotionally, she thought. Even though she'd defended his small-town choice to his grandmother, she protected herself by not letting herself believe completely that he'd stay. "No. But it makes a statement and…"

"You don't trust me." He put a hand on the counter and looked down for a moment. When he met her gaze his own was dark with irritation. "I've already promised everything

I can. One of the most important things you have to learn in medical school is that healing takes time. I'm willing to wait until your doubts are gone." He nodded emphatically. "Now I'm going to see C.J."

Jill wasn't quite sure what to make of that. He wasn't the only one irritated, but she was mad at herself. She'd let her guard down long enough to fall in love and that scared her so much. It wasn't about the flowers; they were just the focus of her fear.

Seeing her little boy run into Adam's arms was a glimpse of what could be and what she'd lose if he let her down. It was always better not to look and hope and have your dream taken away.

The first ring of the phone woke Adam, a side effect of being a doctor. He automatically looked at the bedside digital clock, which read 2:30 a.m. That was never a good thing and he was on call.

He grabbed the receiver and hit Talk. "Dr. Stone."

"Adam? It's Becky."

His sister. This was *really* not a good sign. Adrenaline punched through him and instantly he was alert. He sat up and swung his legs over the side of the bed. "What's wrong?"

"It's Dad. He had chest pain and Mom took him to the E.R. at Mercy Medical Center Dallas."

"How is he?"

"I don't know."

"Did you call Spencer?" Chest pain was his brother's specialty.

"Yes. He's catching the first flight out of Las Vegas. Probably in the morning."

"And Grandmother? You know she's here in Blackwater Lake." And had just told him his father refused to slow down. Damn it.

"I didn't know that." Relief cut through the strain in Becky's voice. "Thank God. I've been trying to reach her on her cell and the calls kept going to voice mail."

"Cell reception is spotty here in the mountains. I'll call the lodge where she's staying."

"Adam, I'm so glad you're there with her. This will be a shock. She puts on a tough face, but she's not getting any younger and is pretty fragile."

"I'll bring her home," he vowed.

"I was hoping you'd say that."

He turned on the table lamp and blinked at the sudden light. "Who's with Mom?"

"I don't think anyone is. I'm driving up from Houston and will be there in a little while."

He knew the drive took a few hours and wondered why she'd waited so long to notify him. "Why didn't you call me sooner?"

"Mom wanted to wait until there was news and I finally overruled her. I needed to hear your voice."

He stood and walked to the bedroom closet, then pulled out a carry-on suitcase. "Is there any information on Dad's condition yet?"

"They're still doing tests and evaluating him. That's all I know—" Her voice caught.

Adam's concern shifted to his sister. "Are you okay?"

"Hanging in there."

"Is Dan with you?"

"No. We couldn't both leave the twins or yank them out of bed and drag them to Dallas. If—"

"Becky?" *Come on,* he thought, *keep it together while you're driving.* The line cut out and crackled with static. "Becky?"

"I'm here. Sorry. The connection isn't great. Dan will

come with the kids when there's more information. He wanted to be with me, but it was best that I go alone for now."

"You two doing okay?"

"Yeah." She didn't ask what he meant. "Counseling is helping. We're both working at the marriage and things are better. Good, in fact."

"You'll be glad to know Grandmother tortured me relentlessly but I didn't spill my guts or your secret. It's driving her nuts."

She laughed as he'd hoped. "I owe you—"

There was a crackle in his ear and he wasn't sure if the call had dropped or not. But he said anyway, "Gotta go, Becks. See you soon."

He hung up and called the Blackwater Lake Lodge, then asked for Eugenia Stone's room. The phone was picked up on the first ring.

"Hello?" The single word was laced with hesitation, fear and dread, just like anyone who received a call at two-forty-five in the morning.

"Grandmother, it's Adam. Sorry to wake you."

"You didn't. What's wrong?"

As a doctor he'd delivered bad news before but never to family. There was no easy way to say this, so he did it quick. "Dad's in the E.R. with chest pain. They're doing tests."

"Oh, Adam—" Emotion choked off her words.

"Cancel your car. I'll drive you and we'll go to the airport together."

"Thank you."

"He's going to be fine, Gram. Probably just high gas pain. But I'll get you to him." He looked at the clock again. "Pick you up in thirty minutes."

"I'll be waiting in the lobby." She hung up.

Adam made a couple more phone calls, one to arrange for another doctor to take calls and one to the Mercy Medical Clinic manager to cancel his appointments that week. He started to dial Jill's number because he badly needed to talk to her. Then he realized that he'd jar her out of a sound sleep and probably C.J., too. As much as he wanted to hear reassurance in that smoky voice of hers, he just couldn't wake her. She needed her rest. He decided to call later when she'd be awake and let her know what was going on.

Twenty minutes later Adam was showered and packed. He left his apartment and walked down the stairs. Jill's porch was at the bottom and he stared at her dark windows and front door, unable to move past. It wasn't only her voice he needed. The hunger to hold her cut through him like a knife, and the thought of not seeing her left an ache in his heart.

Leaving her was like ripping out his soul and when he got back, the two of them needed to have a long talk.

Jill wasn't sure when she first realized something was off but it began to sink in when she and C.J. walked outside to go to school. That was when she recognized that the pattern of sounds signaling Adam's presence was off.

"Dr. Adam's car is gone." Her son opened the rear passenger door and climbed into his booster seat before buckling himself in.

"He must have had a patient emergency," she said, sliding behind the steering wheel.

It wasn't unusual for him to meet someone early at the clinic, but usually it was close to regular operating hours and she heard his footsteps on the front porch when he was on his way. If he'd gotten a call and left in the middle of the night, that meant someone was really sick and she didn't want to think about who it might be and what was wrong.

A short time later she pulled up in front of Blackwater Lake Elementary and put the car in Park. "Do you have your lunch?"

"Yup." C.J. nodded emphatically as he unbuckled his seat belt and slid down from his perch. Then he opened the back door. "We need to remind Dr. Adam that my birthday party is the day after tomorrow."

"Okay, kiddo. I'll do that when I see him."

"I love you, Mommy."

"Love you, too, baby. Zip up your jacket. It's freezing outside."

"I'm not a baby. I'm almost seven." He slammed the door.

Jill smiled as she watched her little man trudge up the sidewalk to where his class lined up, dragging his backpack behind him. It was almost as big as he was, proving that he was still her little man. And he'd grown very attached to Adam, in spite of her efforts to prevent that very thing from happening. C.J. wasn't the only one.

She'd grown accustomed to having the handsome doctor around, listening for the sound of him leaving in the morning and coming home at night, staying for dinner. Making love. And now she wanted to kick herself for being such a witch when he brought her flowers. He'd promised to wait until she trusted, but a part of her believed that she was just too much trouble and it was only a matter of time before he stopped waiting and moved on.

But she didn't want him to give up on her and she'd tell him so when he got home that night.

Since the school was halfway between home and town, she continued on to the grocery store. The weather forecast had a storm moving in and a lot of snow and she decided to stock up on food and get everything for C.J.'s birthday dinner now. Lasagna was his favorite and easily served a lot of people who'd been invited to the party.

After shopping, she drove home and parked the car in the usual spot. A longing swelled inside her to see Adam's SUV in his usual spot beside it. As soon as possible, she would admit to him that she was an idiot, possibly a tad paranoid, and graciously thank him for bringing her flowers.

With a happy smile, she carried her groceries inside, put the cold items in the refrigerator, then left the rest on the counter to deal with later. Then she headed for the marina store to check on things. Brew always had the situation under control, but there was a lot to do with winter coming on.

When she opened the door, the bell over it tinkled. The older man was standing by the cash register and looked up. "Mornin', Jill."

"Hi." She closed out the freezing air. "It's really cold outside."

"Yeah. Can't say I'm lookin' forward to winter. It's harder as a body gets older." He counted the bills in the money drawer that were used to make change if necessary. "This time of year Hildie always threatens to move to Las Vegas where it's warm."

Her chest tightened at the words, a reaction from the part of her that feared being left behind. Then she remembered that Hildie said the same thing every year right around now.

"What did you tell her?"

"That I'd miss her a lot." He grinned.

"You're bad. And a liar." But she smiled at him. "You'd be so lost without her."

"I know it." He shook a finger at her. "But that's just between us. Don't you ever tell her I said that."

"My lips are sealed." Jill looked around the store's interior. Shelves were neat and fully stocked. Displays were in order and sale signs clearly posted on summer merchandise that needed to be gotten rid of. "What's your plan for the day?"

"Got a fishing party comin' in at ten. The same four idiots come every year at this time. A last hurrah, they call it." He shook his head. "I'll get them outfitted and on the way, and then I thought I'd do some work on Adam's boat."

She glanced through the window and saw it under a tarp. He'd be using it when spring came, and the thought made her insides go all gooey and giddy. "Good idea. But maybe you should bring it into the back room and work there. Out of the cold."

"I'll do that." He closed the cash drawer. "Speaking of Adam, what's up with him?"

"Nothing that I know of." Except his pattern was off this morning. Suddenly her glass-is-half-empty attitude punched a hole in her happy balloon. "Why?"

"Hildie had an appointment today at the clinic, but they called to cancel it."

Now the feeling got really bad. As C.J. had pointed out, his car was gone. If he wasn't at the clinic… "Did they say why?"

"No. And when she asked about rescheduling, the girl said she couldn't do that until they heard from him."

"I saw him last night and he didn't say a word about going anywhere." She met the older man's gaze. "He's gone."

"Sounds like it." It was a toss-up whether his voice was more grim or more angry.

Contrary to what he'd promised, he wasn't willing to wait even twenty-four hours for her trust to heal. Self-fulfilling prophecy. He was going to leave anyway, so she'd driven him away. She'd fallen for him and he left without a word, just like everyone else she'd loved. But she'd been so sure he was committed to the community of Blackwater Lake.

"Well," she said, "I guess that's it."

"I know it's hard, but don't jump to conclusions," Brew warned.

That was a tall order. First his grandmother arrives and all but says she's not good enough and then he disappears. What conclusion was she supposed to jump to?

Fear of abandonment was threatening to swamp her like a tsunami. When that first wave rolled back, there was nothing left but a hurt that stole the breath from her lungs. And then something else pressed down on her heart.

C.J. had fallen for him, too. What was she going to tell her little boy? On top of that there was this stupid storm coming and if it was as bad as predicted, his birthday party would be ruined.

When things went bad, they all went bad.

Chapter Fifteen

Two days later the mouthwatering aroma of lasagna and garlic bread filled the house. A few hardy friends who'd braved the still-falling snow had come in Cabot Dixon's multi-passenger, all-wheel drive vehicle to bring birthday presents. The Adam rumor, pieced together from Liz at the clinic and Blackwater Lake Lodge night staff, was that he was visiting his family. Jill had jumped to every possible conclusion but settled on the one that made sense. His grandmother had convinced him to go home.

She hadn't said as much to C.J., just gave him the facts as she knew them. Dr. Adam canceled his clinic appointments and they weren't scheduling any more until hearing from him. So far no one had heard from him. Her son had taken the news well, reminding her that the doctor had promised to be here. But for the last two nights when she'd tucked him in he'd asked about Dr. Adam.

Baking the birthday cake and getting food on the table for

a buffet-style meal had kept Jill busy and she was grateful. At least for a little while there was something to distract her from the pain she knew would only get worse.

She moved to the kitchen doorway and said to the small gathering, "It's on the table. Come get it while it's hot."

"I love lasagna," C.J. yelled at the top of his lungs. With Tyler Dixon behind him he came running down the hall from his bedroom, then navigated a path through the adults who were standing around talking.

Cabot Dixon was in deep conversation with Brady O'Keefe. He was there because Maggie hadn't wanted to take the baby out in the storm. Jill completely understood the need to protect your child. Hildie and Brew sat on the sofa chatting with Ginny Irwin, the nurse at Mercy Medical Clinic. The people C.J. cared about most were in this room. All except Adam Stone.

Jill stood aside while her friends filed past the food arranged on the table. The two boys took their plates, then sat on the living room floor in front of the fireplace and started eating. She was last in line behind Mayor Loretta Goodson. After getting food, they stood together by the front door as all the seating in the small room was already taken.

Loretta took a bite of the layered pasta, meat sauce and cheese. "Mmm. Really good, Jill. I think it's the best one ever."

"Thanks." That was a relief. She wasn't at her best when she'd thrown this together. When your heart was broken, cooking could be risky.

"So," her friend said, mixing dressing into the salad on her plate, "nothing from Adam?"

"No."

"That's just weird."

"Not in my world."

That was a pitiful attempt to make light of what happened

and fell way short of the mark. Jill couldn't believe it had happened to her again and that this time was so much worse. Her heart ached in places she hadn't even known were there. His leaving had left a big hole in her life. And she was so tired from waking at night and feeling the emptiness chase sleep away for good as reality set in.

"I know you've had a string of bad luck," Loretta said sympathetically, "but I really thought he was one of the good guys."

"Me, too." Ginny Irwin moved closer to join them. "Took me a while to warm up to him, but he finally won me over. I'm usually a good judge of character and I was convinced he was here for the long haul."

"I wish I could say it was some comfort not to be the only one fooled." Jill shrugged. "But it's not."

"You talking about Adam?" Brady O'Keefe moved closer.

"What was your first clue?" Ginny's voice was teasing.

"Besides the fact that you three are looking awfully serious?" Brady's brown eyes tracked from one woman to the next. "It stands to reason you're talking about the guy who isn't here. And for what it's worth, I think there's a perfectly reasonable explanation."

"For disappearing?" Ginny sniffed. "I'd like to hear it. The connection was bad when he called to say he wouldn't be in and we expected more information would be forthcoming. It hasn't been."

Brady grinned. "Don't look at me like that. I don't know what the reason is, just said there probably is one."

"He's right," Mayor Goodson said. "Adam has a home here. A medical practice. Neighbors and patients he worked damn hard to become friends with."

Jill listened to them debate the issue. She didn't have the emotional reserves to be on the pro or con side. From her perspective hope only prolonged the pain until she crawled into the acceptance stage where numbness was a welcome relief.

By the time the adults had finally finished eating, she noticed that the boys were horsing around and getting restless. "C.J., why don't you and Tyler put your plates in the kitchen?"

"Okay, Mom." When the errand was finished, he came back into the room and stood beside her.

She put her hand on his shoulder. "I think it's time to open presents and have cake."

He shook his head. "I wanna wait for Dr. Adam."

Jill's stomach knotted and she was afraid she'd lose the little bit of dinner she'd been able to choke down. "Sweetie, I don't think we can wait any longer."

"I know everyone thinks he just left, but he'll be here." The young voice was filled with the will to make it so. "He promised."

"I don't think he's coming," she said quietly. But gentling a blow like that by softening your voice simply wasn't possible.

"You're wrong." The quickness to anger wasn't like C.J. "Dr. Adam said nothing could keep him away from my party."

Jill saw tears gather in his eyes and wanted to cry, too. The hope on her son's little face just made her heart hurt more. She'd wanted so much for his birthday to be perfect and simply couldn't pull that miracle off. It made her unspeakably sad that betrayal would always be the reason C.J. remembered the birthday he turned seven.

She'd remember it, too, because of how hard she'd worked to keep from falling for Adam only to realize it was the forever-after kind of love. But, darn it all, grieving was for tomorrow because neither rain, nor sleet, nor dark of night, nor snow was going to keep her son from having the best birthday she could give him.

"Okay, kiddo. I have an idea. Maybe we can—" Standing by the door, she heard the sound of an engine, but not a car engine. She listened for a few seconds. "Is that a motorcycle? What kind of idiot would ride something like that in weather like this?"

Brady moved to the window beside her. "It's not a motorcycle. That looks like Carl Hayes on a snowmobile. And there's someone on the back."

"Dr. Adam!"

Jill was right behind C.J. when he yanked open the front door. She grabbed his shoulder to keep him from running out into the snow. It looked as though the flurry was letting up, but she didn't want him getting wet and cold. His hopes were already in the stratosphere, but she'd be there to catch him when he dropped to earth. Life wasn't a Hollywood movie where the hero swooped in at the last minute on the back of a snowmobile. Except...

A man swung his leg over the back of the machine. He said something to the driver, who nodded, waved and gunned the motor before moving away. There was something familiar about the bundled-up figure walking up the path. If that wasn't Adam's winter jacket, this guy had one exactly like it.

All his life, Adam hadn't known how lonely loneliness could be until he saw Jill and C.J. silhouetted in the doorway. It was snowy and dark; he was cold and wet. In fact, he'd never been colder or wetter, but the sight of them made it all go away and filled up the big empty place inside that he'd carried around for years.

By the time he got to the porch where they were standing, he couldn't feel his feet. But the smile on C.J.'s face made everything he'd been through to get here worth it.

"Dr. Adam, you came!"

Adam dropped to one knee as the boy moved close and launched into his arms. "I told you nothing would keep me away, champ."

"I missed you so much."

"I missed you, too." *And your mom.* He met Jill's gaze, and the bruised look in her eyes told him she had not believed he would be here.

He had some explaining to do, but before a word passed his lips, she turned and pushed past the people gathered in the doorway. One of those people was Brewster Smith and Adam guessed this wasn't the time to ask the man how his boat was coming along. The scowl was a big clue.

"I thought this was a party." Adam stood, but kept his hand on C.J.'s shoulder. "You don't look happy."

If anything Brew scowled harder. "I told you the first time we met that this is the face you'd get if you hurt my girl."

"I didn't mean—" The tugging on his jacket made him look down.

"Dr. Adam? Did you get me a present?" There was nothing but eager anticipation in C.J.'s expression.

It was nice that at least one person wasn't staring at him as if they'd like to lynch him from the nearest tree. "I didn't have a chance to shop, C.J. But I will. In the meantime I found this for you at DFW."

"What's that?"

"Dallas/Fort Worth Airport." He unzipped his jacket and pulled out a small bag.

The boy opened it and a wide smile split his face. "Oh, boy!" He put the Texas Rangers World Series 2011 baseball hat on his head. "Awesome. Thanks, Dr. Adam."

"You're welcome."

"That was quite an entrance, Doc." Virginia Irwin was on the porch.

"Yeah." He shrugged. "What can I say?"

"You can start explaining. Your only message was to cancel your clinic patients because you were going to Dallas." She folded her arms over her chest.

"Urgent family matter." He was starting to shiver badly.

"And about that entrance you just made? A snowmobile? Carl Hayes?"

"My car got stuck about a mile from his house and I walked there. Carl offered to give me a lift when I told him that I had a very important date." He glanced down at the birthday boy proudly showing off his new hat. "I can explain, Virginia—"

"Call me Ginny," she said. "That was good enough for me. Now, I'm no doctor, but you should probably get out of those wet things and take a hot shower before you catch your death."

"You don't get sick from being cold. Viruses are transmitted in other ways—"

"Spare me the medical lecture."

"I have to talk to Jill first," he insisted.

"I'll let her know. Now march." She pointed at the stairway leading up to his place.

"Yes, ma'am."

"Because I'm feeling charitable toward you, I'm going to pretend you didn't just call me ma'am."

"Understood."

His legs felt stiff and heavy as he walked up the stairs and his hands were shaking badly as he fitted his key into the lock. Inside, he dropped his jacket over a kitchen chair and then went to the bathroom and stripped off his cold, wet clothes. He tried to move faster and was only more frustrated when he couldn't. He was desperate to talk to Jill, to explain what had happened and hope she'd understand. The devastated look on her face was tearing him apart.

When the shower water was hot, he stepped into it. Every instinct urged him to hurry, but he forced himself to stand under the warm spray until the pins and needles feeling in his extremities let up. After that, he quickly washed away the grime from the airport and a long tense day on the road. Ten minutes later he was dried off and his hair was neatly combed. He was warmly dressed in jeans, a long-sleeved shirt and a pullover sweater.

"Hopefully she'll give me bonus points for appearance," he said to his reflection.

It was time to make her understand and he hoped her past wouldn't make her not want to listen.

Adam jogged downstairs and let himself into the house. Everyone stopped talking and stared at him. He raised a hand in acknowledgment. "Hi."

A chorus of greetings followed and he scanned the room for the one person in the world he most wanted to see. She wasn't there and by process of elimination and skilled deductive reasoning, he narrowed down her whereabouts. Without another word to anyone, he went in the kitchen.

Jill was bending over the dishwasher. Any other time it would have been a spectacular view, but not now. Not when everything he'd ever wanted was at risk.

"Jill—"

She straightened and her whole body tensed, but she didn't turn or say a word.

"Ginny said she'd explain that she bullied me into changing into dry clothes." Still nothing. He walked behind her and gently turned her toward him. "Say something. Even if it's to tell me to go to hell. I really need to hear the sound of your voice."

She burst into tears and buried her face in her hands. His heart squeezed painfully at her distress and he gathered her trembling body against his own.

"Don't cry. Please don't. I can't stand it."

"I'm s-sorry. It's just—" After several moments she drew in a shuddering breath, then lifted her tear-streaked face. "No one I love has ever come back."

"Oh, sweetheart—" A lump of emotion choked off his words. He'd put her through hell. It wasn't his fault, but he still hated that she was upset because of him. "Damn it."

"What?"

"I got a call in the middle of the night about my father. There was chest pain and I suspected he'd had a heart attack. I had to go."

"Oh, Adam—of course you did."

"I had to go and didn't want to wake you. In the morning I planned to call from the airport and explain. But men plan and Mother Nature laughs. There was no cell reception. And in Dallas my sister was waiting at DFW. I had to get to the hospital."

"Is your dad okay?"

"Yes, thank God. The attack was mild and there was no permanent muscle damage. It was more of a warning to slow down and take better care of himself. My brother Spencer is on top of that."

"Isn't he the heart doctor?"

Adam nodded. "He's running point on the recovery including diet, exercise, medication and cardiac rehabilitation."

"You should have stayed," she protested.

"They threw me out."

Her eyes went wide. "Why would they do that? I thought they were on a mission to get you back home."

"That's true," he confirmed. "But I was home and acutely crabby."

"You? Mr. Sunshine?"

He loosened his hold but didn't let her go. "There were storms all the way from Montana to the Gulf and I couldn't get through to you. I needed to talk to you, to hear your voice. When that wasn't possible, I pretty much ticked off everyone with my bad attitude. Dad was out of the woods and I was told in no uncertain terms to go back where I belonged."

"Here?" The shadows started to lift from her eyes even though tears still clung to her lashes. "Blackwater Lake?"

"Yeah." He couldn't look at her hard enough. "So I grabbed the next flight out and managed to get in before the storm closed the airport. Although cell reception was still impossible. So I drove through a blizzard. Almost made it, too, until I got stuck in the snow."

"Near Carl Hayes's place, Ginny said."

"That's right." He let out a breath. "He gave me a ride."

"So, like the hero in a Hollywood movie you fought your way through a snowstorm for C.J.'s party?" Her mouth curved up at the corners.

"Letting him down wasn't an option." He willed her to believe his next words. "Or you either. I love you, Jill."

"You do?"

He nodded. "More than I can say. I love C.J., too. Being with you guys is the most important thing in my life."

"I thought you didn't want a commitment."

"When I moved here that was the last thing on my mind and I said some stupid, macho things. I knew you'd been badly hurt and I have a bad track record. I didn't want to promise anything and be another guy on the list of men who let you down. But going to Dallas made me realize something."

"What?"

"I didn't know it when I made the decision to move, but coming to Blackwater Lake was all about finding family. I didn't understand that until meeting you and C.J."

"Oh, Adam—" Her voice caught and she blinked furiously.

"I hope those are happy tears because more than anything in the world I want to make you happy."

"I confess, when you were gone without a word I went to the bad place because it's just where I've lived for so long. A habit." She met his gaze and her own was clear and bright. "I trust you, Adam. I'll never doubt you again."

"Prove it. Marry me and I swear to you that I'll be the best husband and father on the planet. I will never leave you."

"I believe you." She smiled. "Before I give you an answer, there's something you should know."

"Okay."

"Your grandmother told me that I shouldn't be picking out wedding patterns and monogramming towels. She said that Dallas was your home and you'd be returning to it soon."

"Then apparently my bad attitude while away from you changed her mind." He grinned. "She's the one who told me to leave."

"Really?"

"I couldn't make that stuff up." He met her gaze. "I'm waiting for an answer. Please don't keep me in suspense."

"Yes. Yes. Yes." She rose on tiptoe and touched her lips to his. "More than anything I want to be your wife."

Adam returned the kiss until her eyes crossed and her toes curled. He finally came up for air and said, "Blackwater Lake is where I live, but being in your arms is and always will be home to me."

"Dr. Adam? Why are you kissin' Mommy?" C.J. moved closer and looked up.

Adam went down on one knee and Jill nodded her approval to share the news. "Champ, if it's okay with you, I'm going to marry your mom."

"And live with us forever?" His eyes opened wider.

"Yes," Adam said. "What do you think?"

"I think that's the best birthday present ever, Dr. Adam."

"Good. And maybe you should call me Adam?"

"Maybe I could call you Daddy?" The child looked at him, then his mother. "Would that be okay?"

"More than okay—" Jill's voice caught when a speechless

Adam pulled C.J. into his arms. She swallowed hard, then said, "I know it's your birthday, kiddo, but I just got the best present ever. Not only are my single-mom days over, but the three of us together are the family I always wanted."

* * * * *

COMING NEXT MONTH from Harlequin®
Special Edition®
AVAILABLE AUGUST 21, 2012

#2209 THE PRODIGAL COWBOY
Kathleen Eagle
Working with Ethan is more challenging than investigative reporter Bella ever dreamed. He's as irresistible as ever, and he has his own buried secrets.

#2210 REAL VINTAGE MAVERICK
Montana Mavericks: Back in the Saddle
Marie Ferrarella
A widowed rancher has given up on love—until he meets a shop owner who believes in second chances. Can she get the cowboy to see it for himself?

#2211 THE DOCTOR'S DO-OVER
Summer Sisters
Karen Templeton
As a kid, he would have done anything to make her happy, to keep her safe. As an adult, is he enough of a man to let her do the same for him?

#2212 THE COWBOY'S FAMILY PLAN
Brighton Valley Babies
Judy Duarte
A doctor and aspiring mother agrees to help a cowboy looking for a surrogate—and falls in love with him.

#2213 THE DOCTOR'S CALLING
Men of the West
Stella Bagwell
Veterinary assistant Laurel Stanton must decide if she should follow her boss and hang on to a hopeless love for him...or move on to a new life.

#2214 TEXAS WEDDING
Celebrations, Inc.
Nancy Robards Thompson
When she opens her own catering company, AJ Sherwood-Antonelli's professional dreams are finally coming true. The last thing she needs is to fall for a hunky soldier who doesn't want to stay in one place long enough put down roots....

You can find more information on upcoming Harlequin® titles, free excerpts and more at www.HarlequinInsideRomance.com.   HSECNM0812

REQUEST YOUR FREE BOOKS!

2 FREE NOVELS PLUS 2 FREE GIFTS!

Harlequin

SPECIAL EDITION

Life, Love & Family

YES! Please send me 2 FREE Harlequin® Special Edition novels and my 2 FREE gifts (gifts are worth about $10). After receiving them, if I don't wish to receive any more books, I can return the shipping statement marked "cancel." If I don't cancel, I will receive 6 brand-new novels every month and be billed just $4.49 per book in the U.S. or $5.24 per book in Canada. That's a saving of at least 14% off the cover price! It's quite a bargain! Shipping and handling is just 50¢ per book in the U.S. and 75¢ per book in Canada.* I understand that accepting the 2 free books and gifts places me under no obligation to buy anything. I can always return a shipment and cancel at any time. Even if I never buy another book, the two free books and gifts are mine to keep forever.

235/335 HDN FEGF

Name _____ (PLEASE PRINT) _____

Address _____ Apt. # _____

City _____ State/Prov. _____ Zip/Postal Code _____

Signature (if under 18, a parent or guardian must sign)

Mail to the **Reader Service:**
IN U.S.A.: P.O. Box 1867, Buffalo, NY 14240-1867
IN CANADA: P.O. Box 609, Fort Erie, Ontario L2A 5X3

Not valid for current subscribers to Harlequin Special Edition books.

Want to try two free books from another line?
Call 1-800-873-8635 or visit www.ReaderService.com.

* Terms and prices subject to change without notice. Prices do not include applicable taxes. Sales tax applicable in N.Y. Canadian residents will be charged applicable taxes. Offer not valid in Quebec. This offer is limited to one order per household. All orders subject to credit approval. Credit or debit balances in a customer's account(s) may be offset by any other outstanding balance owed by or to the customer. Please allow 4 to 6 weeks for delivery. Offer available while quantities last.

Your Privacy—The Reader Service is committed to protecting your privacy. Our Privacy Policy is available online at www.ReaderService.com or upon request from the Reader Service.

We make a portion of our mailing list available to reputable third parties that offer products we believe may interest you. If you prefer that we not exchange your name with third parties, or if you wish to clarify or modify your communication preferences, please visit us at www.ReaderService.com/consumerschoice or write to us at Reader Service Preference Service, P.O. Box 9062, Buffalo, NY 14269. Include your complete name and address.

HSE11B

Harlequin

SPECIAL EDITION

Life, Love and Family

NEW YORK TIMES BESTSELLING AUTHOR

KATHLEEN EAGLE

brings readers a story of a cowboy's return home

Ethan Wolf Track is a true cowboy—rugged,
wild and commitment-free. He's returned home to
South Dakota to rebuild his life, and he'll start by
competing in Mustang Sally's Wild Horse Training
Competition…. But TV reporter Bella Primeaux
is on the hunt for a different kind of prize,
and she'll do whatever it takes
to uncover the truth.

THE PRODIGAL COWBOY

Available September 2012 wherever books are sold!

www.Harlequin.com

HSE65691

Enjoy an exclusive excerpt
from Harlequin® Special Edition®
THE DOCTOR'S DO-OVER *by Karen Templeton*

"What I actually said was that this doesn't make sense."

She cocked her head, frowning. "This?"

His eyes once again met hers. And held on tight.

Oh. This. Got it.

Except…she didn't.

Then he reached over to palm her jaw, making her breath catch and her heart trip an instant before he kissed her. Kissed her good. And hard. But good. Oh, so good, his tongue teasing hers in a way that made everything snap into focus and melt at the same time— Then he backed away, hand still on jaw, eyes still boring into hers. Tortured, what-the-heck-am-I-doing eyes. "If things had gone like I planned, this would've been where I dropped you off, said something about, yeah, I had a nice time, too, I'll call you, and driven away with no intention whatsoever of calling you—"

"With or without the kiss?"

"That kiss? Without."

O-kaay. "Noted. Except…you wouldn't do that."

His brow knotted. "Do what?"

"Tell me you'll call if you're not gonna. Because that is not how you roll, Patrick Shaughnessy."

He let go to let his head drop back against the headrest, emitting a short, rough laugh. "You're going to be the death of me."

"Not intentionally," she said, and he laughed again. But it was such a sad laugh tears sprang to April's eyes.

"No, tonight did not go as planned," he said. "In any way, shape, form or fashion. But weirdly enough in some ways it went better." Another humorless laugh. "Or would have, if you'd been a normal woman."

"As in, whiny and pouty."

"As in, not somebody who'd still be sitting here after what happened. Who would've been out of this truck before I'd even put it in Park. But here you are…" In the dim light, she saw his eyes glisten a moment before he turned, slamming his hand against the steering wheel.

"I don't want this, April! Don't want…you inside my head, seeing how messy it is in there! Don't want…"

He stopped, breathing hard, and April could practically hear him think, *Don't want my heart broken again.*

***

Look for
THE DOCTOR'S DO-OVER
by Karen Templeton
this September 2012 from Harlequin® Special Edition®.

Copyright © 2012 by Harlequin Books S.A.

HSEEXP0912

HARLEQUIN®

SO YOU THINK YOU CAN WRITE

Harlequin and Mills & Boon are joining forces in a global search for new authors.

In September 2012 we're launching our biggest contest yet—with the prize of being published by the world's leader in romance fiction!

Look for more information on our website, **www.soyouthinkyoucanwrite.com**

So you think you can write? Show us!

SYTYCW0912

The scandal continues
in The Santina Crown miniseries
with *USA TODAY* bestselling author

Sarah Morgan

Second in line to the throne, Matteo Santina
knows a thing or two about keeping his cool under
pressure. But when pop star singer Izzy Jackson
shows up to her sister's wedding and makes
a scandalous scene that goes against all royal
protocol, Matteo whisks her offstage, into his limo
and straight to his luxury palazzo.... Rumor has it
that they have yet to emerge!

DEFYING THE
PRINCE

Available August 21 wherever books are sold!

SADDLE UP AND READ 'EM!

Look for this Stetson flash on all Western books this summer!

A COWBOY FOR EVERY MOOD

Pick up a cowboy book
by some of your favorite authors:

Vicki Lewis Thompson
B.J. Daniels
Patricia Thayer
Cathy McDavid

And many more…

Available wherever books are sold.

www.Harlequin.com/Western

ACFEM0612R